Saffron Skies

Saffron Skies

Gabriel Anthony Lopez

Table of Contents

I

And there was a fire in the sky to the west again. It was a lily she was holding across her chest. Helen's parents passed by the open casket, sobbing. She fumbled through a hymnal as the priest ended the closing hymn, just like the funeral had ended in her dreams. The pallbearers lowered the casket to the ground and placed dirt on it.

Jett did not know what to think of the recent death in Placard outside Houston, Texas. There was a bunch of gossip and rumors at the funeral. The glow of the sunset shone on a nearby lake, and wisps of clouds gathered high in the sky. He was more concerned about tonight's party. It was New Year's Eve, after all. It was a terrible time for a funeral, but Helen was a good school friend who had lost Rebecca Holzwarth, a childhood friend of hers. In about six months, they would be off to college, attending separate institutions. Jett chose the University of California, Berkeley, to study meteorology and biology, and Helen chose Swarthmore College to study acting and music.

The funeral gathering made their way to their cars, and later that day, Helen and Jett found themselves in Rebecca's house again. Jett tried to eat some crackers with cheese but found them distasteful. Helen eyed him from the other side of the front room of the house. She finally motioned for him with her hand.

"So, what do you think?" she said. "Do you think anyone knew?"

"Knew what?" quipped Jett.

Jett shifted his body weight. His shoulder muscles ached from yesterday's football practice and workout. The question annoyed Jett, and he looked in the other direction.

"Well, hello there to you too," said a shrilly woman.

"Oh, hello, Aunt Maria! This is Helen. She was Rebecca's friend," said Jett.

Helen shot a polite smile. She placed the ceramic water glass on the serving table and clasped her hands nervously in front of her black dress. Her lip slightly quivered as she dabbed a napkin on her lips.

"Helen, you look marvelous. I'm sure Jett loves it as well," said Aunt Sheryl.

Helen and Jett both blushed. Jett searched for something to say to get this awkward moment past. Aunt Sheryl was an old-school Hispanic, and she held a rosary in her hand. She was dressed in a complete black funeral outfit. The mourners were gathering for a prayer, and Aunt Sheryl joined them. Jett and Helen stood at the back of the group. He looked at his watch, and it was five o'clock. He planned to ditch the wake and meet his best friend, Peter Vern, for tonight's party.

Jett grabbed Helen's hand and took her through the house, kitchen, and outside. Light snow began to fall. Jett put on his beanie and jacket, and Helen also put on her winter jacket and clothes.

"We are going to meet Peter at a loft on the other side of town," said Jett.

"Is the loft near here?" said Helen

"We will have to walk through the woods and get my car at my Dad's shop," said Jett.

The light snow falling quickly turned into a flurry. Jett and Helen wrapped their arms around each other for warmth against the cold. Jett was looking ahead when he noticed what looked like flames.

"What is that?" said Jett.

"I don't know, but we should stay away from it," said Helen.

Jett started to run towards the flames, intrigued and hoping no one was hurt. Before he knew it, he hit something and landed on his back in the snow. He heard Helen laugh, but then he got up and shook the snow off his clothes.

"What was that?" said Jett.

"I don't know, but watching you fall was funny," said Helen.

Jett's hands started to itch, and he took off his gloves. Both Jett and Helen stared with fear at the look on Jett's hands. The veins in his hands had grown larger and black with orange and saffron in them. Suddenly, Jett and Helen began to lift from the ground. A wind began to whip around them. Jett could hear a low hum, but then it got louder.

"Jett Sanchez! What is going on?" said Helen.

"I don't know, but I wish it would stop, too," said Jett.

Soon, orange orbs began to float around them. They whizzed back and forth and did circles in the sky above them. Jett looked down at his hands. The strange black and orange colors began to course up his arms. Helen screamed. Suddenly, they fall to the ground. Jett reached out to touch where the obstacle had been, but it was gone. The orange orbs were gone as well. He ran further to see if they were gone for good. Nothing was there.

Jett thought about a rational, scientific explanation, but he could think of none. He looked down at his arms and hands. Only an ochre shimmer was left on them. Helen ran up to Jett and sobbed on his shoulder. She was always more dramatic—the opposite of him, he thought. Jett's smartphone began to ring.

"Hello, is Helen Carr there?" said a man's voice. Jett quickly put the call on speaker. Helen stared at the phone while the man repeated his question. Helen brought her ear to the smartphone, hoping the man would not hear her breath.

The call started to break, and then silence fell on Jett and Helen. Snow began falling in a blizzard, and Helen panicked again. They still had not reached Jett's father's shop or Peter's place. Jett kept a small flashlight on his key chain. He turned it on, and it began to shine through the snow. He could tell in the distance that the snow was already starting to abate..

Jett heard a throb and rumble and looked around the woods again. The sound came closer until he saw a vehicle's headlights. Helen stood to face the car, but whizzing sounds began to fill the air as she did. They were the sounds of bullets.

"Run and get to the trees," said Jett.

Helen took off running, and Jett grabbed his smartphone. He wanted to capture the perpetrator who was firing bullets at them, so he snapped a picture and then ran. Jett and Helen were safely in the woods again, and they kept moving to the other side, where the center of Placard was and Jett's father's shop.

Jett and Helen went inside the shop. It was silent, and the lights and heater had been turned off. Jett went to the other side of the main room to turn the heater on, left his father a note that he was going to Peter's for the night, and told him about the party he planned to attend that night.

"What do you think was going on back there?" said Helen.

Jett shook his head.

"I don't know or want to know," said Jett.

"Whoever that was who shot bullets at us knew us! Do you think they saw what we saw?" said Helen.

Jett reasoned that it should not be addressed if he could not explain it, at least for now. Jett's phone rang, and he hesitated to pick it up immediately. The screen had been cracked during the encounter, but it was still working. Jett looked down to see who it was on the other side of the line. It was Peter.

"Jett, where are you? The party is blazing right now," said Peter.

"I'm at my dad's shop. There was a hold-up," said Jett.

"Well, what happened? Was it Helen?" said Peter.

Helen looked to the side and slowly walked away from Jett, standing behind one of the shop's counters. Jett wanted to hang up the phone; he knew where this conversation with Peter was going, too. He wrote a note for his father and put it on the cashier's register.

"It's kind of serious, Peter," said Jett.

"Well, what happened?" Peter said.

"I'll tell you when I get there. Over here, Helen, we'll use my truck to get to Peter's place," said Jett.

Peter was a year older than Jett and was already in college. All of Peter's friends were in college, too. Helen did not speak on the way to the party. Night fell as they drove there. There were already plenty of people at the party when Jett and Helen walked in through the door.

When Jett and Helen saw Peter, he was drunk. Jett scanned the room for more of his friends. Tim and Steve were chatting with a college freshman named Hilary Potter in the corner. He didn't want to deal with Peter right now.

"Hey, buddy, glad you could make it!" said Peter.

The television was on, and several people were looking at it. Outside, there was a veranda with some more people. Peter never really kept his parties low for Placard.

"Did you hear of that new investment opportunity with Silicon Valley?" said Peter, trying to start a conversation.

"That is nice, Peter, but I must talk to you about something. Can I see you in one of your rooms?" said Jett.

They reached the room. It was clean. Movie posters adorned the walls.

"So, Jett, did you hit it off with Helen? What's the news?" said Peter continually in a loud, drunken fashion.

"Something happened, Peter. Helen and I were shot at, and a group of people chased after us in cars. We ran into the woods for safety," said Jett.

"No way, that's so cool," said Peter.

Tim and Steve would be better off talking now, but Peter was his best friend, and this was his party. He needed to get through to Peter. Jett and Peter chit-chatted for a while. They were in the room when they heard a loud bang, and the emergency broadcast system went off in the main living area, where some of the people attending the party were having fun. At first, they ignored it. Then, the loud bangs continued, bringing Jett into the living area.

"Let's go, Peter," said Jett.

The loud bangs gradually gave way to the sound of explosions. Screams from the veranda were heard, and Jett and Peter quickly went out to help. There was no one there to help, though. They had been taken, and it was then that the fire filled. Jett looked up at the sky. The flames in the sky cast an unearthly saffron color down to the town. More explosions were heard, and then they saw one. A fireball careened towards the town center. It hit, and some power went out on the other side of town.

"We need to go back inside to know if anyone else has heard about this," said Jett.

When they went inside, some of the female party-goers were crying as they had hit the floor with the explosions. Jett hit the TV. Helen walked up to him. The TV finally came back on the national news service. A reporter was reporting in a nearby city.

"All residents and non-essential personnel have been told to evacuate," said the reporter.

Behind her, flames danced across the skyline. Army vehicles were already visible. One of the lieutenants took the reporter's mic.

"Folks, what you see is being treated as an attack, not an act of nature or God. This is from somewhere not of this world," said the lieutenant.

"So, it's true," said Jett to Helen.

Jett had hoped it would be just his group of friends' secret. Now, this was about something more than just him and Helen. They were selected for some reason, perhaps even chosen.

Helen looked frightened and a little dismayed. She began to put on her coat, but Jett held his hand up to stop her. She looked him straight in the eye.

"I'm going home. I need to see my family," said Helen.

"But it's not safe," said Jett.

Jett relented, and he was surprised at Helen's stubbornness. She moved toward the door and went out into the now-fiery skies. Jett gathered everyone and told them they could go home or stay with them for shelter. Most had left Peter's house except one or two party-goers. The clock struck midnight, and the flames raged with orange and ochre embers.

He put Peter to bed as he could not stay up any longer through the night. Timothy Matthis, Steven Harold, and Hilary Potter stayed beside each other, and Hilary took an extra room while the boys took their place in the living room. Jett did not feel like sleeping. Instead, he made coffee and sat at the central kitchen oval table.

Sitting quietly while the others snored, wondering when evacuation orders would be given to Placard. The clock struck 6:30 a.m. when he noticed an unusual sight. The fires above Placard stopped, and he could only see the fires from the fringe of the city. The sun began to shine over the hills to the west and down through the streets of Placard. Instead of seeing the stillness of the Sun, it seemed to belch out the same flames and fireballs surrounding the city.

"What time is it?" said Timothy Matthis.

"The flames are gone, but this time, something is different about the sun," said Jett.

Timothy went over to the window and saw for himself. Steven also looked out of the window. Hilary awoke and grabbed a cup of cold coffee. She may have been hungover from the night before.

"Where's Peter?" said Hilary.

"He's still asleep," said Jett.

The doorbell rang in the loft. Jett went to the door. First, he looked through the peephole. He found three soldiers with weapons outside the door.

He turned around and motioned to the others to return to their rooms. He was always good at charades. He did not want to open the door, but thought about Helen and the others. Maybe this will solve their predicament. He opened the door slowly but assuredly.

"Are you Jett Sanchez?" the soldier asked, a large weapon strapped across his chest.

"I am," said Jett.

"You need to come with us. It's a matter of national security," the soldier said.

"But wait, I don't know anything?" said Jett.

"You are Jett Sanchez, correct?" the soldier said.

"Yes," said Jett.

"Then, you need to come with us," said the soldier assertively.

Jett took a few steps outside the door and closed it behind him. For a while, the soldiers stared at him through black Oakley sunglasses and shifted the weight of their weapons. He thought of his family and the great times they had together. Indeed, this wasn't the end, but it was in his best interest.

"What is this all about?" said Jett.

By then, they had passed three black military jeeps, and Jett took a back seat in the last one. The soldier revved up the engine and briefly talked into his smartphone. He looked back at Jett.

"This is a matter of the world's end," the soldier said.

II

Jett felt the rush of wind from the Gulf of Mexico. He was somewhere sandy and salty. The soldier undid the cloth that had been tied around his head. He looked out, and to his amazement, what he saw was clear, but more massive amounts of blue flowed back and forth from the anomaly.

He felt pressure everywhere on his body. His spine felt like it was starting to compress, and like his lungs were collapsing. A soldier handed him a pressure suit.

"Where's the equipment to separate us from what this is, so we can put on the pressure and containment suit?" Jett questioned.

"No, time for that. And no one knows what it will do without us taking action right now," the soldier said.

"It?" said Jett.

The soldier smiled. His ink-black hair shone in the light, refracting from the anomaly. He was getting into his suit when Jett noticed hearing aids in his ears. Zipping up the suit, the soldier ushered Jett into his.

"My name is Sergeant Mack Hitts. We have different names based on what you are seeing. Some call it the Fog, the Judgement, and others our Requiem," said Sergeant Hitts.

Jett felt better and was more comfortable now that he was in the suit. He was not more comfortable around Sergeant Hitts. Jett was from a long line of hippie-like families, originally from New Mexico, and had settled in Texas. He had heard stories that they had seen better days. The sergeant looked ahead, spoke into a Bluetooth-like device, and consulted some scientific instruments.

"Were there any people injured? Were there any deaths?" Jett further questioned.

"Walk over here," said Sergeant Hitts.

Some cars stood motionless in the streets. Jett's hair on his arms and head began to stand up, and what he was about to see frightened him even more than the signals his body was giving him. All of a sudden, he was staring at a woman with her mouth gaping open, like she was about to scream. Her scream went unheard as Jett ran into her, her body cold and stiff. There were hundreds, if not thousands, more victims along the Strand.

"Don't touch them," said Sergeant Hitts.

That was said after his suit made contact with the woman. He looked around. The victims were everywhere. How could the sergeant take this? He started to panic. Sergeant Hitts ran over to him.

"Listen to me, man, you've got to keep it together!" said Sergeant Hitts.

Jett started to curse; he did not care about the sergeant or his duties. He wanted to get back home and see Helen and his family. That was until something darted behind the sergeant.

"There's hope," said the sergeant while grabbing Jett's arm.

Jett was more inquisitive about what darted behind the sergeant. It looked like a blue, iridescent orb. What is with orbs lately? He gave a tap on his suit. The orb was above them. Suddenly, rain fell on them.

It was a ton of running as Jetta and Sergeant Hitts walked further across the Strand past victims of the Fog, the Requiem, or whatever. More orbs began to dance, flowing like water. When they flew, they flowed like water from a waterfall. Passing by more victims, they eventually made their way out onto the cold beach.

The anomaly was silent, but the orbs were not. Each had its distinctive hum, it seemed. Sergeant Hitts tried to swat some away from his face and body.

"Why do you wear those hearing aids?" Jett asked randomly while looking at the anomaly.

"For research purposes. The orbs have their distinctive hum if you haven't noticed that yet. Other instruments malfunction when they are near them. So, we have to resort to hearing aids and recording the sounds to identify them," said Sergeant Hitts.

Jett began to notice other exceptional things about the orbs. As they passed him, everything became blurry, and his vision was clouded with a blue hue. His hearing became muffled, and a tingling sensation went throughout his body. The orbs bounced back and forth from the sand or cemented ground to the sky. Sometimes, they were even playful. Dancing whimsically and beckoning towards him. At other times, Jett would feel apprehensive when the orbs seemingly lash out and transform into ovals or oblong shapes.

Sergeant Hitts noticed all these interchanges between Jett and the orbs. He noted them in a blue journal, recording the sounds the orbs made and Jett's playful conversations with them, much like a human would with a dog. Jett's scientific side was getting the best of him now that he was beginning to forget what had happened in Placard and what had led him here.

"Having fun?" said Sergeant Hitts.

"Yeah! These orbs are amazing! What exactly are they?" Jett said.

"We are unsure about our guests. The hum they give off resembles a symphony. Each orb in the group, like an orchestra, has a different instrument to play and note," said Sergeant Hitts.

"Who are they, and what are they humming to?" said Jett.

Sergeant Hitts took out his recorder and a scientific instrument. He touched the recorder. It began to play back some hums from the orbs. Some orbs quickly dove into the waves, crashing on the beach. Some danced in the air, but a couple separated and came near Jett.

One put himself right in front of Jett's face. Sergeant Hitts moved over to where Jett was and began recording the unusual hum that the orb was now emitting. The orb threw itself back a couple of yards from Jett, then suddenly sped up and entered Jett's body before Sergeant Hitts could knock Jett out of the way.

Jett was brought to his knees. Sergeant Hitts brought out a small flashlight to look into Jett's pupils. They were dilated. Sergeant Hitts immediately called for backup from his unit.

"We need an extraction, now!" said Sergeant Hitts.

Jett knelt there motionless. His eyes were unblinking, and his senses diminished. A hum from Jett's body could be heard, and Sergeant Hitts took out his recorder again.

"What happened?" a soldier said when they got to him.

"An orb went into him. It put him into this—" Sergeant Hitts trailed off, unnerved by the scene.

"He looks like he is in some kind of trance," said a soldier to Sergeant Hitts.

"What is Command saying? Where should we take him?" said Sergeant Hitts.

The soldier began to radio in to Command, but the signal became static, and the wind started to pick up along the beach. The orbs had stood at a distance since the lone orb had entered Jett's body. Sergeant Hitts and the soldier picked up Jett's body and put him in the back of a covered truck.

"The weather is getting bad," said Sergeant Hitts to the soldier.

"There was nothing in the weather report; only the anomaly was picked up on radar and other scientific measurements," the soldier said.

The waves began to grow more prominent and crashed on the beach. Despite the window, the victims did not move, anchored in place by an unknowable force. Some signs from the shops along the Strand swayed back and forth, tossed to the wind. Hitts held on to Jett. He was taking note of everything when suddenly Jett's lips moved and uttered a sound.

"Hang in there, Jett!" said Sergeant Hitts.

The command's base was at Moody Gardens. They worked inside the pyramids, and what initially brought them to the base was the attraction the orbs had to the Gardens. In the presence of the orbs, the animals and trees of the pyramids remained unaffected, but there were also victims at Moody Gardens.

Sergeant Hitts took Jett's body and placed it in a sizable cylindrical-shaped container. Some soldiers went over to Jett with medical equipment and other unusual devices. The other soldier who took Jett's body and Sergeant Hitts to Command brought Hitt aside for comment.

"Sergeant Hitts, you know, it's unlikely Jeff will live," said the soldier.

"And, you're who…again?" said Sergeant Hitts.

"Corporal Corporal Lance," the soldier said in a youthful, masculine tone.

"It looks like it is psychiatric, too, and not just medical. Like he is in some catatonic state," said Sergeant Hitts.

"Is the General here?" said Corporal Lance.

"He's coming in from Houston," said Sergeant Hitts.

Sergeant Hitts was walking over to the container holding Jett's body when the ground beneath his feet began to move, everywhere. Sergeant Hitts had heard about how earthquakes in California resemble waves or shifts, but this one was different. It was like the earth was alive and wanted to swallow him. He grasped a pillar in the building.

Cracks began to appear in the welcoming center. Sergeant Hitts kept his eyes on Jett. He said a prayer that Jett would live and not die in that pathetic state that those damn orbs put him in. Jett was their hope, and now the earth continues to move.

A reporter suddenly appeared on the television. Images of lava, fire, and rock spewing from the earth filled the screen. The photos came from the east of Houston, and the images from downtown were frightening. High-rise buildings were collapsing, homes were being torched, and cars flopped around like nothing. The sky had an eerie glow. Jett had seen this before in Placard and during the initial carnage. Sergeant Hitts had seen this color before, during his evacuations of people, and with the arrival of the anomaly. It was the color of different shades of orange.

Why did this color matter? Sergeant Hitts did not know. Why not marigold, orange, or something? He ran over to Jett. At this point, Jett was foaming from the mouth, and the medical personnel were working to get an open airway. No one here could utter why they needed Jett so severely because the General was not here yet.

"Can you get an open airway on him?" said Sergeant Hitts.

"Positive, sir. But we do not know for how long," said a nurse.

Jett suddenly grabbed one of the nurses and threw her across the room. He screamed. He screamed so loudly that Sergeant Hitts covered his ears. Jett then said something that he would never forget.

"I love you, Helen!" said Jett.

"Who is Helen?" said Sergeant Hitts to a soldier from his unit who had been with him since the beginning.

"I think she may be one of his friends from Placard," the soldier said.

"Well, he's hanging in there if he remembers her correctly," said Sergeant Hitts.

"What are those things that entered his body?" said the soldier, pointing at the X-ray screen and monitor.

"I don't know, but we may have more. Look!" said Sergeant Hitts, pointing to the television.

The fires raged on Houston's eastern horizon, and more orbs emerged from the large cracks in the ground. These were red. They began to strike the ground, and when they did, lava would spew, a hole would rip open in a street, or a couple of buildings would topple.

"Sergeant Hitts, the General," said a soldier.

"Well?" said Sergeant Hitts.

"He's dead!" said the soldier.

Despair washed over Sergeant Hitts; he was the highest-ranking officer here, with all these corporals around him. Jett continued to scream. Sergeant Hitts looked across the street at swaying traffic lights in the wind. The traffic lights were stuck on red. Some orbs were there, but they kept their distance. That's when Sergeant Hitts came up with an idea: red light.

"We need someone to go to the street and retrieve the traffic light, then rig it to shine it on Jet," said Sergeant Hitts.

"Yes, sir," the soldiers replied.

Corporal Lance and some soldiers ran outside to position themselves to take down a traffic light. The medical personnel sedated Jett. After some time had passed, Corporal Lance and the other soldiers placed the traffic light in front of Jett and set it to the color red.

Sergeant Hitts was still trying to absorb what these things were. They were not entirely friendly, and the situation with them could have turned deadly. The medical team, Sergeant Hitts, and others stepped back from Jett's catatonic body.

"What do you think the red light will do, Sergeant Hitts?" said Corporal Lance.

"I expect his body to absorb and interact with the orb somehow," said Sergeant Hitts.

Jett's body began shaking. He opened his mouth and began to glow blue. Was the orb coming out?

Still in the container, Jett clawed at it. He screamed, and the blue orb that shot out of him bounced off the container and soared into the air with the other orbs. The medical team rushed to Jett while he was trying to catch his breath.

Sergeant Hitts ran up to Jett. Jett had a dazed and confused look on his face. Jett looked at these hands.

"Where's Helen?" said Jett.

"Who's Helen? You mean, you're a friend from Placard?" said Sergeant Hitts.

"Yes," groaned Jett.

"Jett, I need to know if you saw anything. Anything at all?" said Sergeant Hitts.

" I-I don't know. Everything was white where I was. " It felt like I was floating in the air," Jett said.

"Why do we need Helen?" said Jett.

"Love. " That's what these creatures want, love," Jett said.

He almost took that information collection, if he would call it that, as a slap in the face. He had lost so many people. All for *love*?

"Do you know how we can communicate with them? Control them?" said Sergeant Hitts.

"You don't control. They control you here now that they are on Earth. We can communicate with them, though," said Jett.

"Like, how can we communicate with them?" said Sergeant Hitts.

"Through color, like you did, or through glyphs. There's an alien ship in the marshes close to here," said Jett.

"So, it's true. These things are not from Earth," said Sergeant Hitts.

"Yes," said Jett.

"Okay, people, we've got a job to do. We've got an alien ship to find," said Sergeant Hitts

Jett began to get upset. All he wanted to do was see Helen and his friends. He sucked up his anger, though, and took a deep breath and stood up. Some medical personnel assisted him as he was a bit wobbly.

Coming down from the steps leading up to the container, Jett looked at the television. There was devastation everywhere on the east side of Houston, and the scope of the catastrophe was getting bigger. Pretty soon, it would hit downtown and the entire city. His stomach hit the floor.

Taking a sip of water by the doors leading to the outside, Jett suddenly saw more soldiers making their way to the command door. When the soldiers parted, he saw the figures. It was Peter and Helen. He ran up to them as fast as his body would let him.

"Helen, you're safe!" said Jett.

"I know. Thanks to you, they managed to get some of us out of Placard and into a safer area," said Helen.

"What do you mean by safer? This is more like the epicenter, ground zero," said Jett.

"The fire and the orbs have spread, Jett," said Peter.

"What about my Dad?" said Jett.

"It was just us they could find and take for now," said Peter.

Jett's heart hit the bottom of his stomach again. He did not know where his dad was now. He had to remain hopeful, though.

III

Jett looked at the drained marsh and the ominous-looking, cavern-like hole. He, Helen, and Peter had to wear a specialized suit to enter the alien ship. When they entered, the walls appeared as smooth and black as onyx. Despite the humidity level surrounding the vessel, it was dry inside, and the three of them did not have to worry about slipping.

Why did the army want them inside the ship? Jett did not know. He thought he was the most qualified, believing this was more of a scientific matter and an emergency. Peter was a purely business type of guy, destined for the Wharton School in Pennsylvania. Jett knew Helen was here because of the revelation when the orb entered his body. The army surmised a part of him *needed* her here. Some hallways went around what Jett, Helen, and Peter could not figure out, but some army scientists were following them.

One was named Hunter Clark. He specialized in almost everything except meteorology and biology, which Jett was interested in.

Jett was standing on another level when he saw blast marks coated with white dust on the vessel's black walls. He tried to clear the area, and the dust fell to the floor. He moved before the army personnel, so Clark and the others did not see that someone had tampered with the ship.

"Any clues, Hunter?" said Peter.

"None so far. What about you, Jett?" said Clark.

"Um, nothing, really," said Jett as he shook off the white dust.

Helen was quiet. Jett did not want her to be with him. It was dangerous. But time was in short supply, and the orb encountered was proof that Helen had a purpose here.

"What about you, Helen?" asked Clark.

"Since I do not have Extra Sensory Perception or any skill other than acting. I think the walls are artful and delicate," said Helen.

When asked to do something more than acting or the arts, Helen always had a biting tone. Jett liked her, though, despite her foibles. Maybe that is why she was here: to overcome some of her shortcomings.

The longer they stayed on the ship, the more Jett felt they were at some religious site. The army personnel had remained quiet since they had been on the vessel. They were all huddled together when suddenly they saw a white light coming from somewhere down the black hallways.

"Halt!" said Clark.

The white light was bright and looked like sunshine at first. But then, the light began to coalesce. Jett squinted through the dark. He recognized what he saw. They were orbs. He held Peter and Helen back with his arm as the army personnel moved toward them. They had flashlight-looking devices, which Jett surmised were used to communicate with the orbs. The red-traffic-light technique worked, so this could do the trick. Clark was the first to send out a message with the flash-like devices.

"Clark is sweating. That's not good," said Peter

As soon as Peter said that, the temperature rose where Jett and the three of them stood. It was so hot that it made them run backward. The orbs began to jump and dart around in a fashion Jett had seen in the organization of migratory birds. Was it a language? They continued, and then a blinding flash of light came, and the visors of Jett, Peter, and Helen. When the visors adjusted to the new light circumstances in the vessel, Clark and a couple of other military personnel were gone, and so were the orbs.

The personnel left were hysterical. Clutching their ears, covering their eyes, and holding their heads. One of them was still in a kneeling position, grinding his teeth. Jett ran up to him, as he was the furthest in the group.

"What do you see?" said Jett.

"I saw, I saw them—" said the soldier.

"Who?" said Jett.

"I saw an old man carrying some fire," said the soldier.

Jett opened up the soldier's eyes and placed a light in them. They were distant and dilated. Helen and Peter were tending to the others.

The soldier grabbed Jet and began to gasp for air. Jet felt the terror of him. He looked like he was dying.

"I saw you, Jett! Are you him?" said the soldier. Then, like that, the soldier gasped his last breath. Jett tried to feed the soldier some oxygen from his suit, but it was useless.

Jett suddenly saw an old man holding a brazier with a fire. The older man looked at him with dark brown eyes. The old man's black hair waved in the wind as he moved through a forest. Jett felt calm around the old man but knew this was only a fleeting encounter. He shook himself out of the moment.

Jett ran over to Helen, who was sitting against the vessel's black walls. She tried comforting one of the men, holding his ears and screaming. Jett searched in her pockets for a sedative the army may have given her. Nothing.

"Make it stop!" shouted the soldier.

"What's your name? Helen, it's important that we get through to them, so we do not lose them to whatever power this is," said Jett.

"Tommy Hicks," said the twenty-something soldier.

Tommy continued to scream, but Jett took a cue from the other soldier and placed his hands over Tommy's ears. He stopped screaming. And began crying in relief.

"It looks like it worked," said Helen.

"Yes, it looks like it did," said Jett.

Peter came over from treating the other soldiers. He was sweaty since he had been holding the soldiers to administer the sedative to a lot of them. Peter looked through his kit to find a sedative to give to Tommy.

When Peter gave Tommy the sedative, Tommy looked at Jett, his eyes wide in amazement. He started to clamor at the ship's walls.

"You are him. You have come to take his place. You have come to guide them, to set them free, and to rule," said Tommy.

"What is he talking about?" said Peter.

"I don't know. I hope the sedative continues to work, though," said Jett.

"We need to radio in some help," said Peter.

"I got the radio," said Helen.

Helen started to adjust the radio to find the frequency, but all she got was static. She tried again and again, but there was nothing. Frustrated, Jett began taking off the headset from his suit.

"What are you doing, Jett? You don't know the environment in here," said Helen.

Before undoing his headset, he checked the gas meters and other scientific instruments for the oxygen level and other gases. They were normal.

"Screw this," said Jett.

"Jett, don't!" said Peter and Helen simultaneously.

He took off his helmet and breathed in and out cold air. It was cold now. Jett gave them the OK sign, so they knew he was doing all right. The cold hit him like a punch to his chest. The temperature must have changed since they saw the white light and orbs.

Jett looked around the hallway and took some steps past where the white light had been. He could see the outline of nothing. There was nothing but a seamless black hallway. There must be something in the center that he knew.

Jett was desperate for some answers. He put some of his upgraded smartphones, which the army gave him, up against the wall in front of him, behind him, and further down the hallway. Progress was finally made. A white substance began accumulating on the phone, so Jett knew some energy was flowing through the vessel. What was more interesting, thought Jett, was that it seemed biological.

Peter approached him with some notes scribbled down by a soldier. Peter held them up to the flashlight on his headset. The environmental conditions were changing rapidly now. Water was beginning to collect on the paper and make it wet.

"What do you have?" inquired Jett.

"A soldier wrote what he saw or was in his mind when the white flash went off, and the white orbs appeared. It looks like some glyphic writing," said Peter.

Jett looked at the papers. He had not seen writings like these since his family had told him extensively about their ancestors. Jett was Hispanic, but he did not know how knowledgeable he was about what seemed to be things outside his expertise in hard science.

"They looked like Mesoamerican glyphic writing. I can't tell whether they are Olmec, Mayan, or something else," said Jett.

"Aztec, maybe?" said Peter.

"I'm not sure," said Jett.

Jett looked over to where Helen was with the soldiers. They all looked sedated, and she continued her efforts with the radio. Jett held the paper of the glyphic writing up to the onyx-colored walls of the vessel.

As soon as he did this, lines shone through the wall, and Jett removed the paper. The vessel's walls had somehow picked up on the writing. The lines were white at first, then kept changing color.

In front of Jett and Peter, an outline of a door began to form. The light then began emanating from the outline. The brightness of the light made Jett shield his eyes. And then, it was gone.

"This door has secrets," said Peter.

"That's obvious. And I am determined to find out what they are," said Jett.

Whisps of cold and humid air came from the store. Jett stooped down to see if he could push the door open and make further progress into the vessel. He pressed the door, and the light around it intensified; glyphs appeared when his palms touched its surface. The door opened with an eerie whisper.

It opened from the bottom and top, and when Jett looked into the vessel past the door, he saw a single pinpoint of white light in what appeared to be the center of a vast room. Jett stepped forward, and his boots felt heavier here, as if the gravity was stronger in the room. Peter followed, and he began to cling to Jett.

"Quit holding on to me, Peter," said Jett.

"Do you think that's an orb?" said Peter nervously.

The pinpoint of light began to pulsate. It seemed to grow distant and closer at the same time. Jett and Peter only made it so close to the light before the gravity in the room gave way, and they began to float upward to what they did not know. Peter began to float upward past Jett.

"Jett, help me get down from here!" said Peter.

Jett jumped and lurched backward to where he believed the gravity was stronger. Peter fell to the side of him. Jett, then, saw her.

She was a young woman in a long jade-colored skirt and white cotton shirt, holding the pinpoint of light like she was tending to it. Her hair was black and wild but beautiful. Her skin and eyes were a warm brown, and she had a twinkle in her eyes. She was brown, and he found she was lovely. The light began to shine brighter and brighter like the sun.

A roar erupted in the vast room, sounding like water rushing in. Wetness formed on Jett's face, but the young woman stood there holding the light. Peter grabbed and pushed Jett to get up, moved back to the hallway, and closed the door.

"Peter, we've got to go. It sounds like water coming!" said Peter in terror.

The sound of the water was terrifying, but Jett found the young woman's calmness and delicacy more frightening. "Was she a prisoner here?" he thought. He instinctively ran to her, but was instead propelled backward to where Peter was in the room, towards the hallway.

Jett and Peter were in the hallway when the vessel began to shake, and the roar of the water grew louder. The ship was large enough to hold vast amounts of water, so Jett needed to get the young woman out of the room.

"I come to destroy and give rebirth," the young woman said.

Jett was stunned. She was not just any ordinary young woman. Was she an alien, though, Jett? Jett kept looking at her. She finally held the light in her hand and enclosed her hands around it, smothering it.

Jett felt her power while he was in the room. He managed to get to the hallway with Peter. He was despondent. He had never seen such beauty and ferocity in a single person. He heard the radio and then thought of Helen.

"Jett, Peter!" said Helen. Helen hugged Jett. Helen's hug felt distant, even though she was still close. The young woman in there had taken his breath away.

"What did you guys see? Anything," said Helen.

"Um, we saw a light, a young woman, and we heard the roar of water," said Jett.

"And, well, did it mean anything?" said Helen.

"Well, the glyphic writing Peter showed me worked, and this ship is part biological," said Jett.

"Sounds like you did all you could. The soldiers have come out of their daze or stunning or whatever," said Helen, giving Jett a peck on the cheek.

Jett loved it when Helen was that close to him. He remembered past summer days in Placard when the two of them spent time together and had grown close enough to share a kiss. Now, Jett felt accomplished. He was bothered by what he had seen. He had never seen such a young woman as beautiful and strong, as strong as enough to destroy the sun.

While they were collecting their thoughts, the radio came back on, and they heard the voice of a soldier. Helen ran over to where the radio was and grabbed it. He looked at Peter and Jett to make sure they knew what to say through it.

"Anyone, there! This is Command. Anyone there?" said the voice.

"This is the unnamed group that was under the command of Sergeant Hitts," Helen said.

"Was? Where is he?" said the voice.

"Who is this first? He didn't make it. Several of the group didn't make it. But the other civilians and I did," said Helen.

"This is Lieutenant Genero. Captain Schill wants everyone to return to Command. We couldn't contact you because we believe the anomaly rolled in—the Fog, the Judgment, etc.—the situation was intense for a while," said Lieutenant Genero.

"Got that. " We'll pack up and head out of the vessel," Helen said.

Jett came over and hugged Helen. She was stressed, but she had made Jett proud. The vessel lurched again. Jett, Peter, and Helen readjusted their flashlights and exited the makeshift command on the salty marsh. When Jett was near the door and about to exit, he halted. He felt a presence as if someone or something was looking at him. He turned to look. In the darkness of the vessel, he could see what appeared to be the outline of a large, black cat roaming the ship.

IV

When they arrived back at Command at Moody Gardens, they were greeted by more military personnel and refugees. They had a new superior, Captain Meno, to whom they reported. Jett and the others jotted down their accounts in the journals given to them. Jett was the first to be interviewed by Captain Meno.

The two sat in an unused room off the side of the main room, which housed the military and refugees. Captain Meno was more serious than Sergeant Hitts. He was well-groomed, with a bald head and a cleanly shaved appearance.

"So, who was this young woman you wrote about, Jett?" said Captain Meno.

"You are getting to the point," said Jett.

Captain Meno raised an eyebrow. Jett was not nervous—not yet—and he politely nodded back at Captain Meno. He did not return the casual gesture. He just looked at Jett and then crossed his arms. And he coughed into his hands and rubbed them together, trying to warm them.

"What did you think of the vessel?" said Captain Meno.

"It has many biological components, despite its solid appearance on the inside and out," said Jett.

"What else did you observe and encounter for the record?" said Captain Meno.

"When the encounter with the white orbs and the disappearance of Sergeant Hitts and the other personnel happened, some of the other soldiers began to write down glyphic writing," said Jett.

"And?" said Captain Meno

"It opened a door. And that's when I saw the young woman," said Jett.

Captain Meno huffed slightly as he stood up from his chair. He flipped through his small notebook and sighed. There was something he was not telling.

"I'm sorry for the loss of your men," said Jett in a firm voice.

A lieutenant approached Captain Meno to tell him some news. They kept their voices hushed and turned their bodies away from Jett, who heard more refugees straggling in from everywhere.

Captain Meno suddenly stood beside Jett, his eyes fixed on him with curiosity. He had a computer pad and asked Jett to enter his name and birthdate. This was the most formal the army had gotten with him since Placard.

"You've been assigned to the Anomaly on the Strand again. You will observe and take samples, and Peter and Helen will join you. They are being briefed as well," Captain Meno said.

Jett was nervous now. Why him? Others were more capable anywhere in the world.

"Is there any other news from around the country?" asked Jett.

"There have been sightings and encounters with orbs in Los Angeles, Chicago, New York City, Miami, and other cities. You get the picture," said Captain Meno.

Captain Meno went off with some lieutenants, a corporal, and other personnel. Jett just sat in the chair he was sitting in for a while. He had to go to the Anomaly at one o'clock military time. He did not like using military time, which made him nervous. He made it to the doorway of the main room and looked around him.

In the distance, he saw a man in a black suit with black sunglasses, pursuing him through a newspaper. Jett thought nothing of him except that he was smoking, which was strictly forbidden at Command. He then turned and looked at Jett, staring at him.

Jett felt he had seen him before, but did not know where. The man appeared agitated as Jett approached the main room. Jett walked toward him. Jett took note and then moved toward the military personnel in the room.

He was about to turn his back on the man when he saw what was on his hip. It was a gun. Jett turns back to walk quickly toward Helen and Peter, who are on the other side of the room. Jett was not looking for trouble. How did the man gain access to Command? It was a restricted area.

A crowd of people came in front of him. Then, someone bumped him from behind. He did not want to look to see who it was, and he did. It was the man.

He was face-to-face with him. He was about Jett's height, with stubble on his face and black hair. The coat on his suit covered the gun.

"Sorry, I dropped something," the man said.

"Oh, no problem," Jett said, looking at the floor.

Jett saw what appeared to be a credit card. He bent to pick it up, and the sharp edges cut into his skin when he did. He winced in pain.

The man just stared back at him. Letting even more people run into him. He took Jett's hand and wiped off the blood on the tips of Jett's fingers with a handkerchief.

"We know who you are," said the man bluntly.

He then let go of Jett's hand and put the handkerchief in his pocket. Some refugees ran between him and the man, and another group came. By then, the man was gone.

Jett held his handkerchief and went to Peter and Helen on the other side of the room. Peter was sitting down, eating a sandwich, and watching the news with Helen, who was having soup.

"What happened to your hand?!" exclaimed Helen.

"Oh, nothing. I just helped the captain move some boxes, and I accidentally cut my fingers," said Jett, lying through his teeth.

"Some bandages are in the first aid kit across from you," said Peter.

"Thank you. We are all going to the Anomaly today at one o'clock. " We will need all the rest we can get," Jett said.

Helen had never seen the victims of the Anomaly, who by now were not just on the strand but also in Houston, New York City, and throughout major metropolitan areas in America. Her job was to assess whether any changes had occurred in the victims' environment or bodily states and analyze them for any damage they may have sustained in their current state.

"Have any of the victims moved?" said Helen to a corporal.

"None that we know of. They all have been frozen like fish in a winter's pond," said the corporal.

"All are paralyzed by whatever or whoever's act of terror occurred," said Helen as she went amongst the countless victims. Some other personnel joined to help her.

"Corporal Balco, over here," said Peter.

Peter was assigned to collect samples of sand, earth, and cement. Jett looked over Peter's shoulder and found that many areas Peter had tested looked like they had been set on fire. No one had witnessed fire on the Strand. The area had remained bitingly cold. It was also recorded that the weather would change to uncomfortably humid and hot within hours. This is where Jett came into the picture.

He was on the Strand to analyze the atmospheric composition of the anomaly. And gather any meteorological data about where the Anomaly, the fire, and the orbs could go next in the world. So far, it has been contained in the United States.

Jett walked onto a rock outcropping called a jetty. As he drew closer to the Anomaly, the air thickened, and the water became increasingly placid until the sound of the waves ceased altogether. When Jett reached the end of the jetty, he could see the Anomaly. He took out a scientific instrument and took a sample of the air. He could have almost cut the Anomaly with a scalpel if he had had one. When he took the sample, he could have sworn the Anomaly, which went on for miles and miles, had groaned.

He placed the samples of the Anomaly into a case strapped around his waist. The samples were being returned to Command, and Jett rejoined the others. When he was halfway down the jetty, he saw a faint figure. The heaviness of the air gripped Jett's chest. The Anomaly seemed to move in his direction.

"Corporal Balco, the Anomaly is moving," radioed in Jett.

Jett began to run, but he seemed to be running in place for some reason. He started clutching his chest. He looked around him, and all he could see was the Fog.

It seemed like Jett was in a dream, and he began to scream. Then he felt a sense of peace come over him, and the faint figure transformed into an older man. The older man was cloaked in grey and hooded, and Jett looked at him closely. There was an owl perched on his shoulder.

The owl hooted and hooted, spreading its wings. It turned its head, and the older man motioned for Jett to come closer to him. Jett then saw a temple and the vessel they had been in on the salt marsh.

He then saw boulders in a jungle, completely round boulders. The howls of monkeys filled the jungle. The trees rustled behind him, and he could see fainter figures of what looked like men. Then, his journey ended.

The older man was still before Jett, but when Jett stretched his hand to touch him, the older man and the owl faded from his vision. The heaviness of the air still surrounded him. Jett then realized the immediacy of danger. His radio began to sound off in the stillness of the air.

"Jett, this is Corporal Balco. Please respond," said Balco.

Jett continued to run, holding the radio to his ear and mouth. Somehow, he knew it was not his time to die. He reached the end of the jetty in about thirty seconds.

He jumped on the Strand. He was glad he reached solid ground. He was so pleased that he ran out into the street, only to stop by the motionless victims.

Jett felt someone grab his arm, and he jumped. It was Helen. Her soothing features calmed his racing heart. She looked tired, though.

"Jett, what happened?" said Helen.

"The Anomaly started to move when I took the samples, and I saw someone—an older man," said Jett.

"Who? There was no one there. The corporal and everyone were watching you from afar before the Anomaly rolled in," said Helen.

Helen and Jett made their way back onto the Strand. Peter joined them with his samples of the dirt, sand, and cement that they knew the Anomaly had touched. They walked to where the corporal and the other military personnel were on the Strand.

"How did it go with your sampling, Peter?" said Jett

At first, Peter did not respond. He looked a bit too clean for scouring around in the dirt. Jett looked at him more closely. His sample instruments contained nothing. Jett turned to look and talked to Helen, the corporal, and others to exchange information. When Jett looked back at Peter, there were substances in the instruments.

"I didn't find much, I think," said Peter with a polite smile.

Some of the military science personnel took Peter's samples. The military began issuing official name badges to be worn on civilian clothing. Jett, Helen, and Peter went to the corporal for their badges.

"Helen Stunt, Peter Kline, and Jett Sanchez," the corporal said.

"That's us," the three said.

They each placed their badges on the containment suits they were wearing. The corporal gave them some additional clothing to wear. Helen put her hair in a bun.

"Helen, what about your observations of the victims? " Any changes from what we have recorded so far?" said a military science officer.

"None, except for a lot of condensation on their skin, and some seemed charred by a fire or something, while others — the ground has begun to give way beneath them," said Helen.

"Thank you for your notes," the science officer said.

"Corporal Balco, what did you think of the movement of the Anomaly?" said Jett.

"God's wrath and judgment are again on the move. I guess. It took out a flock of birds, hundreds of people, hundreds of people, as you can see on the beach," said Balco.

Jett looked out to the beach, where there was seaweed, rocks, and dead fish. Now, he saw the recently dead birds. Jett had a hunch that the Anomaly that continued to paralyze and kill was something his grandmother had told him once.

"I think the Anomaly is some kind of pollutant," said Jett.

"What do you mean?" said Balco.

"I mean, the government has declared this not an act of God, but there is something ancient about the Anomaly when you are up close to it," said Jett.

"Go on," said Balco.

"I've only heard it from my grandmother when she wanted me to become a doctor, and I read it in a textbook. It is called miasma," Jett said.

"What's that?" chimed in many of the science personnel.

"Well, it's an ancient Greek belief. Miasma had a contagious power over the ancient Greeks. So much so that it had an independent life of its own; it caused death until purged by the sacrificial death of the wrongdoer. Until then, society would be chronically infected by catastrophe," said Jett.

"Is there a more scientific explanation? And why wrongdoing?" said Balco.

"Well, miasma only came to the ancient Greeks when some injustice occurred. It only goes away when the one who has done the wrongdoing has undergone a sacrificial death. Some say this is not from Earth or space or somewhere else, but the culprit is us," said Jett.

"But the culprit isn't us. Does this connect to the vessel?" said a science officer.

"Mythic stuff began to happen in the vessel, so there is some connection. And who knows where myth is from?" said Jett.

"Is there any form of intelligence other than this miasma—or contagion or whatever—something we can communicate with?" said Balco.

"There is something inside the vessel in the salt marsh. I know that for certain," said Jett.

"Thank you, Jett, for your observations, notes, and bravery. We'll take it from here and analyze Helen and Peter's final observations as well," said Balco.

Jett, Helen, and Peter went to a military site to remove their containment suits. While Jett took off his clothes, Helen turned away but occasionally peeked around a curtain. Peter tried to hide his laughter at the two.

"You guys are falling for each other more and more," said Peter, laughing.

"We are not," said Jett as he put on his pants.

"That was an interesting theory you gave to the corporal. What do you think Captain Meno and the people above him will do?" said Peter.

"I started guessing since they debated whether or not it's from Earth or God," said Jett.

"Yeah, some people think it's Judgment Day, you know. Do you think it is?" said Peter.

"I am attempting to fulfill the scientist role and remain scientifically accurate. To say the least, we need more evidence. We need to go back to the vessel," said Jett.

Peter smirked as they walked out of the locker room to meet Helen. Jett looked at Helen, who looked ravishing since she had cleaned up in the women's locker room. Peter was right, it was Judgment Day, he thought. Captain Meno will have more direct orders, data, and conclusions. For now, the three of them got into a military vehicle to the Command and waited for a signal from the higher-up personnel.

V

It was a rainy day at Command. The soldiers attempted to cover themselves, but the storms passing through were almost like hurricanes, even though it was winter. Jett noted this in a journal.

At lunch, the three met with Captain Meno for a briefing. There was nothing unusual about Captain Meno while he sat and talked to them during lunch, but he seemed fatigued, like something was weighing him down. Helen raised her hand the most during the briefing. Jett still had lingering thoughts about why they kept her on the mission. Peter twiddled his thumbs—literally.

"You all will go into the vessel and attempt to get into the large room at the center of the vessel," said Captain Meno.

"Will we have more assistance this time?" said Helen.

"You guys will be given anything you need. We took some readings of the vessel, and a room exists. This is the only vessel we have found on American soil and, for what we know, the world. You need to come back with any knowledge or samples we can gather for the sake of America and possibly the world now," said Captain Meno.

Jett did not like his tone. He shifted in his chair, looking over the graphs and other information plastered on the walls behind the captain. The orbs and the Anomaly have so far been confined to the USA.

"Is there any evidence that the orbs and the Anomaly have spread, Captain Meno?" said Jett.

"Nothing conclusive yet. The US military has been so bogged down dealing with these disruptions that we have occasionally lost contact with our allies and have not received any help. The encounters with the orbs and the anomaly we know affect technology," said Captain Meno.

Peter raised his hand.

"You said we would be given anything we wanted. Does that include money?" said Peter.

Jett felt like punching Peter when he said what he did, so he did—his arm. Peter was also conniving and, to put it bluntly, an aspiring businessman who could get killed. Maybe Peter was there because they needed him to manage the money and deal with possible communications. Captain Meno looked at Jett.

"You are all here for a reason," said Captain Meno.

Helen clapped her hands, and Peter let out a whoop of excitement. Jett instead sat back and sighed. Where were the more qualified scientists? And why him?

When they arrived at base camp before the vessel, the weather had changed again. It reminded him of the weather he and his father would encounter when they went hunting at state parks in Texas. Yet this time, the weather was even more temperamental. Captain Meno had kept to his promise that they would be given anything they wanted. There were more crew and military personnel, and the scientific instruments Jett wanted. Corporal Balco had been assigned to help them inside the vessel.

"Jett, how are you? Since we are already acquainted, I'll get to business," said the corporal.

The corporal was eager, as was everyone. Helen looked at Jett again as she talked to some female personnel helping her put on her containment suit. She was calmer and more composed than Jett. He had too many knots in his stomach, but he did not want to give any sign that he wanted to back out of the mission.

The vessel looked more or less like a flattened muffin. It is almost classically saucer-shaped except with a noticeable base to it. It was more like something Jett had seen in old science fiction movies.

As they approached the vessel's entrance, Jett observed a black ooze tinged with ochre. Jet noted the color mixture. As they entered the vessel further, more colors were noticeable. Everyone acknowledged saffron, burnt sienna, marine blue, forest green, and many more. Jett and most of the crew and military personnel were inside the vessel when they noticed the light from the entrance seemed to get swallowed by the vessel's insides.

"It's darker than a night without city lights in here," said a soldier.

"Where are the lights in here, Jett?" said Corporal Balco.

"There are none," said Jett ominously.

He could have sworn he saw movement when they went deeper into the vessel at a particular moment. It was so real that Helen screamed. Everyone chalked it up to the movement of another soldier who had strayed away from the group.

"Everyone stick together. From my readings, we are almost at the doorway to the great room," said Corporal Balco.

Jett had lost where Peter was in the vessel. He heard someone running, and it was Peter. Jett scowled in the glow of the flashlight he was holding.

"Where did you go?" said Jett strictly.

"I took some samples of that colored ooze. Maybe our visitors are painters. They would appreciate our admiration. I thought," said Peter.

"Peter, did you bring the computer pad with the glyphic writing?" said Jett.

"Yes, I did," said Peter.

All of them stood before the doorway with their flashlights and instrumentation. Peter placed the computer on top of the doorway, and then the pad stayed there to let the sensors work. The doorway began to open.

"Ready yourselves, everyone!" commanded Corporal Balco.

"Yes, sir," said the soldiers in a chorus.

"No need to. Whatever is in there isn't looking for a fight," said Jett.

"But there are victims, and the sky is burning everywhere in America. I am not just going off your hunch," said Balco.

As the computer pad continued to calculate, Peter grew impatient. So, he kicked the door and the computer. Jett wanted to say something to Peter badly, such as, 'Are you going to pay for that when you graduate from Wharton?'

"You didn't have to do that, Peter," Jett said.

The doorway began to open, although more slowly than last time. Jett stepped to the edge of the doorway. Wetness began to accumulate on the outside of his containment mask. It was humid. Jett checked the instrumentation to read the gases, and the amounts were perfect inside the great room. He took off his mask.

He walked halfway to where he had seen the young woman holding the white orb. As Jett looked around him, it was so black and dark that it looked like he was floating again. He could have been floating again. He took out his notebook in the great room. It began to fall, and then it started to float. Before he knew it, he began to float, too.

Balco and everyone followed him. They spread as far as they could until some soldiers began radioing into Jett. They sounded confused.

"Jett, this room seems to go on and on. It's not just a room. My readings go past the length and width of what it is on the outside," said a soldier.

"Stay close, everyone; the water and the young woman could happen again," said Jett cautiously.

Jett remembered one thing he had not looked for that massive black cat or jaguar. He had barely seen the cat. So far, he had not. When Jett thought a light appeared before him, a stone was seen in the middle of the room. There was a faint light surrounding it as well. Peter was standing next to him when this occurred.

"What is it?" said Peter.

"I don't know. It looks like an almost perfectly spherical boulder," said Jett.

"It looks volcanic," said Peter.

"You surmised right," said Balco as he positioned his computer pad over the stone.

Jett then felt a tapping on his left. He looked. There was nothing there. He looked over to Peter, who was talking to Balco.

Helen was busy taking notes of the crew and military personnel interacting with the environment. She was squinting in the dark. All these had tired her, including her eyes. Jett knew that about her now. She was strong, though, to have gone through this until now.

"How are you?" asked Jett as he crouched beside Helen.

Helen smiled gracefully as she thumbed her notes. Her blue eyes still looked like they twinkled in the dark light of the vessel, and her cheeks were rose colored. He always thought she could be the one for him and never wanted to lose her.

"I am more worried about the personnel and the crew. They are my duty," said Helen bluntly.

"Why don't you take a breather?" said Jett, massaging her right arm.

"I must do my work. Captain Meno and everyone—the world—has put a lot of trust in us," said Helen.

Jett had noticed Peter had wandered off to the side of the spherical boulder. Peter had put on some night vision goggles from the military personnel. Despite the goggles, all he saw was pitch black through them.

"Jett, the goggles are not picking up anything," said Peter.

Jett was about to go over to where Peter was when both of them froze in their places. Helen screamed as Jett's hand was still on her arm, and she yelled for him to let go of her. Some of the military personnel noticed and began running over to the group of three.

Peter began to feel something. Something was watching him. He did not know what before he heard a faint whimper, and then he saw it with his own eyes. It was a coyote.

"Jett, are you seeing this?" said Peter.

"I can't put on my goggles or move toward you. I'm stuck," said Jett.

"It's a coyote. I'm adjusting my goggles so that they record," said Peter.

Peter kept looking at the whimpering coyote. It was brown with a slender body and paws that looked like they had moved quickly. Peter was fascinated.

"Jett, can you feel anything?" said a soldier as he tried to free Jett.

"Get over here, Peter!" exclaimed Jett.

The coyote circled Peter, panted, sat up, and howled. When the coyote did this, the sounds of other coyotes in the distance began. Peter's heart started racing, and the life sensors in his suit recorded it.

"I can't see it, Peter," said Jett.

Balco and some others undid the grip on Jet's boots, and he was gradually let loose. Jett stumbled forward, and the floating feeling began again. He looked over at Helen, who was now standing beside Balco. Jett eyed the sphere. The sphere sat there unmoving. When Jett looked at Peter, Peter looked like he was moving his arms up and down to catch someone's attention.

"I'm here," said the coyote to Peter.

"You can talk?" said Peter.

"Mother Earth is always talking. Always in oneness," said the coyote.

"What do you mean? We are here for answers as to why all these phenomena are happening and why thousands of people are dead," said Peter.

"Well, you started it," said the coyote.

"What do you mean?" said Peter.

"Money and power have done it to Mother Earth. You have done it as well. Your friends are different, though. We will be watching you, Peter," said the coyote.

And, with that, the coyote disappeared into the dark, with the howls of other coyotes fading into the distance. Jett slammed into Peter, and whatever held him down let him go. Peter cursed, and Jett felt like the air was knocked out of him. They both scrambled to get themselves together again. There was nothing there but the onyx darkness of the vessel.

Helen ran over to where Jett, Peter, and some soldiers were in the darkness. Helen held Jett's head even though she was starting to float. That's when everyone saw them again. They appeared slowly like sprites from the mythic minds of old. Turning and dancing, they moved over to where Jett, Helen, and Peter were. The orbs began to dance around the volcanic sphere and the group of three.

They started to admit a hum. Jett instantly realized what this meant. It happened the first time they saw them in the Placard. Danger is approaching, he thought.

The orbs looked synchronized in their dances of varied color: blue, orange, red, violet, and yellow. The white ones were not present. They continued to dance until they had almost settled on the heads of everyone in the room. They flickered like candles in a gentle draft in a house. Helen and some soldiers grabbed Jett and Peter and pulled them from the abysmal darkness.

Jett, Peter, and Helen all stood with orbs above their heads. The soldiers brought out some night-vision cameras and began recording. Jett looked up, and there was a warmth to the orbs. Peter started to poke at one, and Helen stood frighteningly still.

"We are picking up the orbs, but not what color they are," said Balco.

"Alright," said Jett.

Looking around the room again, Jett saw the obsidian darkness move. There was something there. He strained his eyes. Jett believed only an animal could make that shape like that. It began to form and move in a fashion that Jett had never seen. Before Jett realized it, a jaguar appeared before him. It came like a vision in smokiness, and it whispered as it approached.

The jaguar eyed him. No one else seemed to notice the jaguar but Jett. He decided to remain quiet and witness as much as he could about the Jaguar. Jett wanted to know if it was real, so he stroked his hand to brush the jaguar's side as the jaguar circled him.

The hairs of the jaguar were smooth and smelled of the tropical wild. The jaguar took its time, then stood before Jett. It's cat eyes catching what was in the darkness.

"Honor, Jett is what you seek. Honor to save Mother Earth. Honor to save your ancestors," said the Jaguar.

"What do you mean? Who are you?" said Jett.

"I am an ancestor conjured by the forces that have been summoned from their long sleep," said the jaguar.

"Do you know what is happening out there? We are here to find out. We need help," said Jett.

"I know what, but only I am told a few things. No more," said the jaguar.

"Are we in any danger?" said Jett.

"Yes, danger is near, Jett. More will happen. The Earth is hurting and responding. Others have awakened and come. Some for various other reasons," said the jaguar.

The jaguar circled Jett and placed a spherical stone on the floor. Its eyes looked caring and intelligent. The jaguar took some steps back from Jett.

"Go to where the spheres are, Jett," said the jaguar.

With that, the jaguar began to fade into a haze. He hadn't realized, but Peter held his arm beside him. The orbs also faded back into the darkness.

"What did you see, Jett? Anything?" said Peter.

"I saw a jaguar. That's what I saw," said Jett nervously.

Jett took notes with Corporal Balco and the other soldiers about what he had seen. They began to make their way out of the great room. When they did, the light and the volcanic sphere faded.

The group collected their things and made their way out of the vessel. When they had reached Command, Corporal Balco noted what Jett and Peter had seen inside the great room of the ship. The Corporal submitted them for psychological testing.

VI

Helen was treating some refugees when Jett walked up to her. It had been almost a week since their last visit to the vessel. They had compiled their data, recordings, and the like for eventual release to Captain Meno.

"Helen, it's time. Captain Meno wants to meet everyone who made the last trip to the vessel. He told us to meet in the room across where the rations are stored," said Jett enthusiastically

Command had been quiet lately. Refugees were trickling in at a slower rate, and the reports of the Anomaly, the orbs, and the fire were less frequent and destructive. Jett had quickly composed his findings from the trip to the vessel. He spent the remainder of the day wandering around the Moody Gardens complex, but everything was closed. It was a cold and blustery February day when they met with Captain Meno. Peter looked overly prepared as he walked into the room. He had a calculator and some data sheets with him. Helen had her journal and Jett as well.

"Everyone, that is a job well done, the last time you visited the vessel," said Captain Meno.

Jett brought his hand down on Peter's shoulder in a congratulatory manner. Jett wanted to congratulate Helen, too, but she was on the other side of the room. Corporal Balco was also with them in the room as a representative of the group that went with them.

"It was amazing what we could find out this time," said Corporal Balco.

"I agree with you, Balco. These orbs appear alive and intertwined with the vessel's environment. But how they interact with the Earth's environment is unclear," said Captain Meno.

"What was concluded about the hallucinations or visions Jett and Peter were having?" he asked inquisitively.

"Yes, we did some psychological testing on Jett and Peter, and the results came back inconclusive. For all we know, Peter and Jett were having or receiving visions," said Captain Meno.

"What about the volcanic sphere we saw? Were you able to see it in the recording?" said Peter.

"We were said to have obtained a recording, Captain Meno, and it appears it revealed they have an origin. At least we know something that looks like them on Earth and where they are," said Captain Meno.

"What are the spheres?" said Jett.

"Our analyses show they resemble and could be the sphere rock from Costa Rica. They are an ancient artifact of a local ancient culture," said Captain Meno.

"What do they do?" said Helen.

"That's the thing. There are a variety of speculations. Some include the more outlandish speculations, such as that they are from aliens, Atlantis, etc. We need to return to Costa Rica with some of them," said Captain Meno.

"Will the Costa Rican government let us examine their artifacts, considering the high global tensions?" asked Peter.

"Yes, they have agreed on a condition that we do not bring anything that will harm their people or anything within their borders," said Captain Meno.

"So, what do we need to do?" said Jett.

"We must take precautions to decontaminate ourselves when we board and exit the planes on the journey to Costa Rica. And, other restrictions," said Captain Meno.

"When do we leave?" said Helen.

"We leave as soon as possible. We need to gather as much data, information, and resources as possible before the next series of events with the Anomaly and the orbs. Any further questions?" said Captain Meno.

No one raised their hand. Jett wanted to ask if there was any speculation about the visions or hallucinations he and Peter had. Captain Meno looked preoccupied, though, so he let the questions go.

***

It was cold at the airport as they boarded a military aircraft. Helen was huddled with Jett, and both were bundled up in coats. Peter stood alone, although he was the first on board the aircraft. The flight to Costa Rica was expected to be uneventful, so Jett brought a pillow to sleep on. He pulled down the shades to the window as the plane lifted off and zoomed higher into the sky.

A guide awaited us when we got off the flight from Houston. He was an American professor from the University of Houston hired to assist Jett, Helen, and Peter. They piled into a taxi and took off toward the museum.

"I am Professor Clements, and I am here to assist you in your efforts with the spheres," he said.

Peter seemed distracted, playing a game on his iPhone. Jett and Helen rattled off their so-called credentials to Professor Clements. When they finished speaking, he gave them a weird look.

"So, you guys are just kids?" said the Professor quizzically.

"Yes, we are about to graduate from high school this summer," said Helen.

"So, why did the military ask you guys for help?" said Clements.

"There was no one else. People were evacuating, dying, or did not know what was going on," said Jett.

"And, what makes you an expert?" said Clements.

"I plan to major in biology and meteorology at Berkeley," said Jett.

"I plan to attend Swarthmore College and major in theatre," said Helen.

Peter remained quiet, and the Professor gave them a wide smile. They were driving on the streets of San José, the capital of Costa Rica. When they reached the hotel, the professor helped them grab their luggage.

"So, this is your place. It is near the Museo Nacional de Costa Rica. It's a couple of miles by car. I'll take you there," said Clements.

Everyone thanked Professor Clements except for Peter, who was still on his iPhone. The professor's presence did not console Jett. He knew they had a job to do, but it still irritated him that he was picked for this mission.

When Jett was in his hotel room, he called his father while Helen and Peter were downstairs having lunch. No one picked up the phone. He tried a couple of other family numbers, but they all went to voicemail. Jett could not get it out of his mind that this was some setup or worse.

Peter and Helen returned from lunch, and they spent the remainder of the day taking car rides with one of the guides that Clements had left them with at the hotel. Peter looked more relaxed than usual, as if nothing had happened. Helen, as always, was the best person to have for company.

At night, Jett lay awake thinking about what the jaguar had said. It wasn't a hallucination, he thought. It had a special meaning, though, he thought. Whatever is happening, everyone is involved now that he knows of it in his life.

Jett was looking out their hotel window at 2 a.m. when he saw it. He saw the fire surrounding San José. He was paralyzed with fear. He saw the little traffic in the city's streets stop in the middle of the night, and people were looking at the sight in the sky. Commotion was heard throughout the hallway. The hotel was filled with the sounds of people leaving their rooms. Jett decided to investigate.

He cautiously opened the door of the room while the others slept. Some women were crying, and a man was hurriedly grabbing his luggage. There was a hotel attendant at the end of the hallway, and he decided to talk to him.

"Have you seen what has happened in the sky?" said Jett.

"Yes, the Costa Rican government asked for help from the United States and other governments to supply some kind of aid and force," he said.

"Can you tell me more?" Jett inquired.

"There's no more information. It all came out over the radio before every radio stopped transmitting," said the attendant.

Jett needed to wake up the others and contact Command and Clements. They needed to get to the spheres and go back to America. Maybe the fire would disappear from the sky above San José.

"Peter, wake up!" commanded Jett.

Peter groaned and put the comforter over his head. Jett punched his side. He let out a groan again, and then he sat up in bed. He looked at Peter angrily.

"What is it?" said Peter.

"The sky, Peter! It's on fire like it is back at home," said Jett.

"What?" said Peter.

Helen stirred in her bed, got up, and walked over to Peter's bed. Her messy hair made her look all the more attractive to Jett. Peter looked like he couldn't care less about everything that was going on around him, but he looked more concerned by the moment.

"We need to get to Professor Clements," said Helen boldly.

"Right, and how do you expect us to do that now that everyone is running for their lives?" said Peter.

"I have a small radio that somehow came with my luggage. We could try to radio in Professor Clements," said Jett.

"That sounds like a plan," said Helen.

Jett took out the radio from his luggage and turned it to the frequency for contacting Professor Clements and Costa

Rican officials and personnel. In the message, he clarified that the situation was dire and that they must move now.

It was 6:30 a.m. when Professor Clements was seen on the hotel's steps. Jett and the others met him there with their scientific instruments and other items. They were to take samples of the spheres and mix them with elements of the vessel and the Anomaly.

"Good morning, Professor," said Jett.

"Good morning, everyone. May we get to it?" said Clements.

By the time they got to the museum, the city had received further evacuation orders, and there were rumors of the Anomaly rolling in from the ocean on Costa Rican beaches on the Pacific side. It was dark when they were in the museum, and Clements had to turn on the lights. They made their way over to the spheres.

Helen was the first to take her sample of the sphere and mix it with the elements they had found at home. They waited for a reaction to show up in the test to determine whether or not there was evidence that the spheres were related to the vessel and the Anomaly. Jett went next with his samples and calmly waited for the results.

"So, do you think there is anything to this assumption, Professor Clements?" said Peter.

"Not every person in this profession of anthropology, archaeology, and history, but some say we do not know even why we are here or where we are from when you get down to the nitty-gritty," said Clements.

Peter huffed. He did not like the answer as it flew in the face of his reason. They continued to chat when Helen noticed a smell emanating from their testing kits, which were holding the combined samples. She covered her face, as did the others, as the scent quickly entered the museum.

"It looks like it reacts," said Clements.

"There is a reaction with samples taken from the vessel and the Anomaly, I would say," said Helen.

"Well, looks like we have fulfilled our duty," said Peter.

Peter had the radio turned up, and suddenly, a broadcaster appeared at high volume. The broadcast was in Spanish, so the Professor had to translate. He began to look worried as the broadcast continued.

"What are they saying?" said Jett.

"Everyone needs to shelter in place or move to higher ground," said Clements.

"We can't. Command's personnel will be waiting for us at the airport," said Peter.

"Well, wait. I am looking through Captain Meno's notes. We must take as much as possible if trouble arises," said Helen.

"Can we take one of your spheres?" smirked Jett.

"I'll have to check with the museum, but sure. Please do what you need to do. People are relying on you," said Clements.

Museum workers arrived to take the spheres to the airport. The shelter-in-place orders had limited the chaos on the city streets, but not by much. When they arrived at the airport, Command was ready for them. Jett looked back at the Professor. Jett felt terrible that they were leaving him. He was in danger.

"Professor, you should come back to the States with us," said Jett.

"Oh, I'll be fine," said Clements.

As they boarded, Jett looked up at the sky. The fire had encircled the city. Not much time was left before the city would be cut off from the rest of the world. Some emergency planes were landing and taking off as well. People were clamoring over one another every time an airport official came near them. When Jett was inside the plane, he noticed the panic on the pilot's face. He decided to look out the window at the sky above them. From nowhere, some orange orbs descended on the airport.

A siren went off at the airport. As police officers and what Jett could tell were the first contingents of the US military, who got more people aboard planes, the orbs began the dance of death. The orange orbs pulsated violently and erratically. When they neared a person, the orb would lift the person off the ground and then slam them back down to their death.

All that mattered for a time to Jett. Helen grew close to him as people began to scream. He held Helen, knowing it would all be over soon. That is when he saw the white orbs coming from inside the plane they were on, and everything faded from sight.

They were in midair somewhere over the Gulf of Mexico when they woke up from whatever caused them to fall unconscious. Most passengers were still knocked out, and Peter was, too. Jett and Helen, however, were awake. Jett wanted to go to the cockpit but knew he could not because of security precautions. Some flight attendants and men were at the door of the cock pit, banging on it.

Anxiety grew within Jett, and then he remembered he had taken a testing kit on board with him and had not left it in the cargo. He took it out and released whatever was in the tube. The smell wafted its way through the plane. Suddenly, the doors of the cockpit opened. A co-pilot fell over onto the floor. A woman shrieked when she saw this, and Jett got up from his chair to see what was going on and asked if he could help. The smell had done something. So, he walked further to the cockpit with the tube. The plane's lights went on and off, and he heard cheers as he reached the cockpit. All the pilots had awakened. After several hours, they were back on track and landed in Houston.

VII

Sleeping had never felt so good to Jett after he landed in Houston. He spent two lovely days in his cot in the main room at Command. There was no privacy. Command had grown since it was first established. Even though there was no privacy, Command brought order to a chaotic world, which was soothing enough to keep Jett asleep. He opened his eyes to the alarm one afternoon around 2 p.m.

"What is it?" said Jett.

"It's me, Jett! Peter!" said a voice.

Jett rubbed his eyes, attempting to work through the grogginess of waking up in the afternoon. It was Peter, all right. He was in full army gear, though.

Jett looked him up and down as he held his hand up to block the sunlight, obscuring his vision. His boots were nice and shiny, and he had a new name badge. It said Vern in bright red letters. Peter threw him a uniform.

"The corporal says we need to keep up to date with identifying ourselves," said Peter cheerfully.

"Alright. Is there anything else?" said Jett.

Jett did not want Peter to bother him now. He was thinking about something too much. He did not like that he had seen the orbs again. And he was frightened that there was a correlation between the spheres and the vessel.

"We are going to put one of the spheres we got in Costa Rica inside the ship to see if it does anything or means anything," said Peter.

"Do they want us all to smell?" said Jett.

"There is only one way to find out," said Peter encouragingly.

"Where's Helen?" said Jett.

"She's in the shower," stated Peter.

Jett looked at the long lines of people all waiting for food toward the area where Command had set up a cafeteria with rations. The cold had abated some, and it was more like a cool spring down in Texas. Turning around in his cot, he looked outside and saw the anomaly, pale and fog-like as ever.

"I'll get up and meet you with Captain Meno," said Jett.

"Alright," said Peter.

Jett stepped behind a screen to put on his uniform. When he stepped back into the main room, he saw a man in a suit.

It was a black suit. The man looked similar to the man he had seen before, except he attempted to make direct eye contact this time. This did not unnerve Jett, as military personnel around him provided him with rations and clothes. Something about him was unwelcoming, threatening, and peculiar for the current circumstances.

Jett walked over to the women's section of the main room to find Helen, and the man disappeared into the crowd. Helen was in a towel, about to go behind a screen. She smiled and looked at Jett like she was glad to see him.

"I've seen the new uniforms. We are moving up in the world," said Helen.

"Yeah, we even got new name tags," said Jett.

"How was your sleep? It looked like you needed it when we got off the plane from Costa Rica," said Helen observingly.

"It was wonderful. I have never felt better. However, we need to get to Captain Meno about the sphere. Peter says he wants us to put it inside the vessel," said Jett.

"We might as well get to work," said Helen as she adjusted her belt on her uniform.

Later in the day, Jett approached Captain Meno about putting the volcanic sphere into the vessel. Jett had been nervous about this mission, so he did not want to ask Captain Meno any questions or encourage him initially.

"Jett, we will have our best on the mission with you and the others," said Captain Meno.

Jett smiled a nervous smile but took heart in Captain Meno's words. He had more questions now than on previous missions. Were they making progress in figuring out what was going on? Maybe they would not need him in the future.

At the end of the week, Captain Meno gathered everyone who had been on a mission to the vessel and gave a briefing. Some new personnel from Washington, D.C., assisted him. Perhaps they would not need him for long.

"Everyone, today we go into the vessel with the volcanic sphere. It will be worked on mostly at night," said Captain Meno.

There was some murmuring in the group as Captain Meno continued to explain the mission. Jett, Peter, and Helen will first go in with Corporal Balco, the personnel, and the crew. Captain Meno said they were not expecting much from the vessel except for the funny smells. Everyone laughed.

As Jett approached the vessel a couple of hours later, he noticed the ship had changed in its dark, onyx color. It had become so black that parts had somehow turned blue and purple in the lightning from base camp. He stepped into the vessel with Captain Balco and the sphere ahead of them. It was pulled by some soldiers taken from their routine duty.

When they reached the doorway again, they held up a computer pad with the glyphic writing, and the doorway opened. It was pitch black in the great room again. Jett and Balco stepped into the seemingly floorless room. It was only a room because of the echoes they occasionally heard faintly.

The soldiers looked around and then at Jett and the others. They looked amazed. Jett motioned them with his hand to go a bit further.

"If you go about two feet more, that is where the other sphere was," said Jett.

The soldiers released the rope, harnessing the large sphere. It did not make a sound when it settled on the area where the last sphere was. They waited for a biological reaction to the sphere. Instead, they heard a whirling sound like the sound of air in a wind tunnel. Helen shrieked and held on to Peter. Jett hated it when she did stuff like that in front of him. The sound increased until the air sped up and picked up the sphere, and glyphic writing glowed brightly in the darkness. Peter took out his specialized camera and took some photos.

The vessel jostled and lurched. Jett waited for the biological reaction. The equipment they brought with them began to turn off and on randomly. Finally, there was a sizzle from under the sphere. Jett bent down to look. A black and orange ooze dripped from underneath the sphere. Jett got up and moved back, but then he hit a console of some sort, and some lights went on throughout the vessel. The spheres were tied into the vessel's inner workings, he thought.

Jett took down some notes, and they stayed inside the sphere for a while. They analyzed the new console they had found and wondered if it could pilot the ship or turn it on somehow. Helen observed the military personnel and crew's reactions to the environment.

"Jett, do you think the Anomaly will know what we have done here?" said Helen worryingly.

Jett thought for a moment. His original theory was the miasma theory, which suggested that the Anomaly was, at the very least, originating from somewhere. The vessel was included in this theory. Now, whether they are from the same place is a different story.

When they exited the sphere this time, a jubilant crowd awaited them. Jett turned around and found out why. The vessel had risen several feet from the salty marsh. Jett leaped down from the vessel, followed by Peter. Jett grabbed Helen as she got down from the vessel. Captain Meno ran up to them with a face full of exhilaration.

"That's a damn good job, everybody! What did you do in there?!" said Captain Meno.

"Well, sir, there was a biological reaction, and the sphere is tied to the inner workings of the vessel," said Jett.

"Oh, you mean we owe Costa Rica some money for using their artifact?" said Captain Meno jokingly as he shook Jett's hand.

While talking to Captain Meno, Jett noticed a man dressed in casual, civilian clothing over the captain's shoulder. He did not look roughed up in the least bit, at least not like the refugees. He was slick and clean. Jett instantly remembered him as the guy he kept bumping into at Command.

Jett then noticed Peter walking up to the man. Peter had some notes in his hand and some rations. Jett stayed in front of the captain, halfway listening to what he had to say, when he noticed a woman dressed in an army uniform looking through Peter's backpack, which he had left near his cot.

The man noticed Jett looking at him and gave him a smirk. And, with that, he grabbed Peter and brought a knife to his throat. The woman ran up to him, handcuffed Peter, and brought him to his knees. Several other civilian-looking women and men ran through the main room, throwing gas bombs at everyone. In no time, the room was filled with smoke and a sedative gas.

Jett ran over to his cot and found a gas mask. He found another to give to the captain, but he was knocked out and had hit the floor by then. Jett saw the man and woman take Peter, but Peter resisted. Jett took this opportunity and threw some water where the woman would step. She slipped and lost her grip on Peter. The man immediately noticed Jett. He brought the knife so close to Peter that Jett thought he was going to cut him.

"Jett, you should have stayed hidden," said the man.

The woman got up and swiped at Jet with her fist. Jett ducked and smashed his fist into her stomach, bringing her to the ground. Jett knew he had to move quickly, but he must ask who this man was.

"Who are you? And why are you doing this?" said Jett.

He gave Jett that same wide, evil grin as more gas bombs went off and threw Jett a picture. It was a picture of him, his dad, and his mom. The man showed him a tattoo on his right arm.

"I'm family; don't you get it?" said the man.

Jett slipped the photo into his pocket and lunged after the man holding Peter. The man let go of Peter and grabbed a piece of debris left on the floor. He thrust it at Jett, who moved quickly. Jett wanted the man to get captured, but the military personnel and crew were busy calming the refugees.

Jett managed to get close enough to look at the man's tattoo, which read "Sphinx." The other men and women who had brought in the gas bombs had managed to seal off the main room from the outside. Jett needed to get more identification from this man.

He noticed the man was bleeding, and Jett fell to his cot, where there was an unused testing kit. Grabbing a testing kit, Jett charged at the man. And Jett hoped to get his blood sample to end the stalemate. It would help to apprehend who this guy is.

There were further screams from the refugees and some from the military. It appeared that the Anomaly was on the move again and had struck, killing some people outside on the streets. This alerted the man's group, and they quickly began to retreat.

The man noticed the retreat and brought out a concealed weapon at his side. He took the gun, pointed it at Peter, and shot him. Peter fell to the floor with blood everywhere. Jett screamed and wrestled the man to the ground, but the man thrust himself up and away from Jett.

By then, Corporal Balco had gotten to Jett with Helen. Balco took an assessment of Peter, but he was dead. Helen threw herself onto Jett to keep him safe.

"Jett, stop, just let him go!" screamed Helen.

Jett did not want to relent. The man knew who he was. Jett looked over at Peter, who was bleeding. Helen was right; he needed to stop his fury toward this man. The man with the Sphinx tattoo bolted from where he was to the door and towards the vessel with the other group members.

Jett went to his cot and found a first-aid kit for Peter. Some medical staff arrived, and Peter let them take over his medical treatment. Jett knelt beside Peter as he prayed for Peter to make it. The medical staff moved Peter to the makeshift hospital that the Command had in another building.

Some military personnel unlocked the doors to let in refugees caught outside during the fight. The Anomaly was still on the move, slowly creeping past the Strand. Helen was going through a routine outside the main room.

"Jett, who was that person?" said Helen.

"I don't know. He knew who I was, though. I've seen him before," said Jett.

"We need to check how he knew you. I'll see if the captain is awake yet," said Helen.

Jett was not sure what to make of the attack. Had he not covered any loose ends? All he could think about was that he had not heard from his family. Were they OK? Jett went over and got Corporal Balco's attention.

"Corporal, I need you to check the location of my father and family. Here are their details and any other information I think you may need. I think the man who attacked Peter knows something about them. Or else I would not have been found," said Jett.

"Understood," said Balco.

The doctors had to perform surgery on Peter late into the night. Jett and Helen waited outside in the damp hospital room. He had not heard back from Balco, which did not sound good. Jett was also concerned about Helen and Peter; any information about them must be seized and held.

Looking out over the salt marsh, he saw the fire hovering and dancing over Houston. The fire had not turned deadly yet, like the Anomaly or belligerent like the orbs, but they knew it was only a matter of time. Jett clasped his hands together and brought them to his forehead. If only none of this had happened, if only it had not been chosen by whoever.

"Jett, I'll stay up with you all night if I have to," said Helen.

"You don't have to; you need your rest in case something else happens," said Jett.

Jett had a service member bring over two cots for both of them. It was in the morning when they heard the news.

Peter did not make it. Jett cried. He had not cried in a long time. He cried so hard that it made some of the refugees uncomfortable. He did not care. He had just lost his best friend and teammate. Helen gave Jett hot tea as she sat down with him.

"Peter was a great friend. He'll be missed and remembered for all the good he has done in his life," said Helen.

The air was cold, but not as cold as the hurt left to Jett by that man who shot Peter. Jett told Captain Meno and Corporal Balco everything: the tattoo, clothing style, and anything to capture the man. As they walked away from the hospital area, Jett and Helen glanced at the television to see the news. The Anomaly had moved across the Gulf of Mexico to New Orleans and Tampa Bay, Florida. It was everywhere. Captain Meno called over Helen and Jett because they had a job now.

"What's the death toll?" said Jett.

"About 2,000 died when the Anomaly began moving, mostly refugees and some military," said Captain Meno.

"What do we do now?" said Helen.

"We do all we can. Operations managed to track some of our guys' movement," said Captain Meno.

"Where did that lead?" said Jett.

"It leads to New Orleans, Louisiana, on the other side of the Anomaly. We need to get there fast before the Anomaly consumes the entirety of the Gulf of Mexico," said Captain Meno.

"Do you know why that is?" said Jett inquisitively.

"We know that the guy with the tattoo isn't working alone. Since the port of Houston has been removed, all emergency and non-emergency shipments were rerouted there," said Captain Meno.

"So, is this organized crime, terrorism…Why would they attack?" said Jett.

Captain Meno gave him a long, hard look as if he did not want to answer Jett. Captain Meno took out a file in his binder and handed the papers to Jett and Helen. He turned on the projector in the room to show a tattoo of a Sphinx.

"Whoever our Sphinx guy is working with, they are a secretive organization. They are not exactly organized crime or terrorism, but they act with a purpose. We went through the images captured by the security cameras of the attack. All the belligerents had tattoos of Sphinxes," said Captain Meno.

"Have we identified a leader yet? The Sphinx attacker guy said he was family to me," said Jett.

"No, we have not identified a leader, and there isn't much information on the attackers besides the tattoos," said Captain Meno.

"Have you heard back from any of my family, Helen's family, or Peter's?" said Jett.

"Our team is on top of that. It does appear that the Anomaly has continued to damage the area. There have been rolling blackouts, which hamper communication," said Captain Meno.

"But for now, we are asking you two to report to a Command facility in New Orleans. We need you guys to learn everything you can about the attackers and what this means. You guys are our tendrils, so to speak," said Captain Meno.

"What about the vessel? Can we request assistance?" said Helen.

"We can send Corporal Balco and a couple of men with you. The vessel is so far under our control, but that can change at any moment with the Anomaly this close," said Captain Meno.

"Have you thought about moving Captain Meno?" said Jett.

"With over two million lives lost in America as the Anomaly and the orbs spread across the nation, we must take a risk," said Captain Meno.

"I see," said Jett as he looked at Helen nervously.

"If you find my family, tell them I love them, and I'll make it home," said Jett.

"When do we head to New Orleans?" said Helen.

"A plane is waiting for you at the highway we use as an airport. Good luck," said Captain Meno.

Captain Meno handed Jett and Helen some more files and shook their hands. When they exited the room, Balco and some personnel were waiting, carrying their items and other materials. They took the flight during the day to keep track of the Anomaly and any orbs they may encounter.

When they landed in New Orleans, they began unpacking at a Command base camp in the French Quarter. An older captain was heading the Command operations. Balco and the military personnel from Houston got to work while Jet and Helen took a moment to collect themselves outside the base camp. The streets were filled with displaced people, but that did not dismiss the traditional ambiance of the French Quarter.

Helen was wandering the streets of the French Quarter ahead of Jett. She gazed up at the Anomaly that had begun to wrap around the city. Flickers of the fire were in the sky off in the distance. Jett was watching Helen closely when a disheveled man stood before him. He beckoned toward him. Helen was busy talking to some people and taking down notes. The wild-looking man continued to beckon Jett into an old, sorcery-looking shop tucked back from the street.

Jett walked into the eerie sorcery shop. Amulets hung on the walls, and crystal balls lined tables in the shop's center. Dried chicken feet were hung from the ceiling. Stepping on the creaking wooden floor, Jett followed the man to the back of the shop, where the man went into a basement.

Jett was about to enter the basement when he felt someone behind him. He whirled around and found Helen staring back at him. She looked angry.

"What are you doing, Jett?" said Helen.

"This man looks like he knows me. I think he has something to do with the visions," said Jett.

"What is with you and thinking people know you?" said Helen.

"Look, all this stuff has messed with me. I try to deny I have this bulls-eye on me, but I do. For what reason, I do not know yet," said Jett.

"I do not think anyone is messing with you. We need to go back to base camp," said Helen.

"Let's investigate, just this once," said Jett.

"Jett, how about we return to base camp?" said Helen.

Jett grabbed Helen's hand and pulled her towards the basement. He wanted to know if more people were after him and if Command would help him protect himself from other forces.

"Alright, I'll go, but as soon as we notice something does not feel right, we will leave, okay?" said Helen.

"Yes, we will," said Jett.

They began walking down into the damp, cool basement. Cables were hanging from the ceiling. Lights led further down and lit the walls, showing graffiti of different colors. Further and further, they went down until the long hallway they entered to enter the basement opened to a large room with a cathedral-like ceiling.

"Jett, I think this might be a x. There could be dead bodies down here. Let's go," said Helen.

"The bodies are all buried, Helen. No worries," assured Jett.

Jett and Helen were looking around the immense crypt-style room when suddenly the lights went out. One light shone brightly across the room over a desk. A black chair was there, turned around, facing away from them.

"You've been wondering, Jett and Helen, what has been happening?" said a voice.

"Who are you? Show yourself," said Jett.

The chair turned around, revealing the messy-looking man. A parrot was on his shoulder this time. A dog panted at his side as well.

"Helen, we have been waiting for you," said the man.

He approached Helen, placing his arms and hands behind his back. He eyed her closely but not in an invasive way. Curiosity filled his eyes, and admiration. He threw some chicken bones on the table. He pointed for Jett and Helen to look up, and when Jett and Helen did, they saw a chandelier made out of human skulls.

"Helen, come close," said the man.

Helen slightly leaned into him. When she got close, he blew some dust-like substance on her. She took a step back and began to fall to the floor. Jett jumped to her and caught her before she fell. The man then snapped his fingers in front of Helen. She went into a trance. She began to talk, eyes wide open and staring at the ramparts of the ceiling.

"What have you done to her?" said Jett.

"I merely gave her insight into her situation. Don't you know, Jett? She loves you but cannot yet articulate love," said the man.

"Her love?" said Jett.

"Of course, Jett. Everything is about love, and you are about to take a trip with her, too," said the man.

The man snapped his fingers again and blew dust in Jett's face, too. Jett gasped and reached out toward the man, hoping to get to him before the substance took over, but he soon hit the floor beside Helen.

***

Jett woke beside Helen, who was already awake, searching through the forest and abandoned buildings. She looked like she had been looking around the area, and Jett could tell this was not reality. There was something different about Helen. Her hair looked unkept, and she had freckles on her face. Jett pinched himself. He felt the pinch, but something in his surroundings just seemed off the more he peered into the surrounding trees.

"Jett, where are we?" Helen asked frantically.

"Um, we are in some dream-like forest…a hallucination perhaps?" said Jett.

"What was in that dust?" said Helen.

"A drug of some sort, from what I can guess," said Jett, scoping out the surrounding area further.

Jett and Helen moved through the trees and over some boulders. They came to a clearing. The grass was tall and looked like a fresh rain had fallen. Jett looked at the middle of the clearing with Helen behind him.

"Jett, stop!" said Helen.

"Wait, what are you doing?" said Jett.

"I need to go see what is out there. It wants me," said Helen.

"Helen, you are not making any sense," said Jett.

"I am. Look!" said Helen as she pointed to the middle of the clearing.

Helen started to run and point, and Jett looked and found a snake with its head and front body reared up and looking at Helen. She stopped in front of it. The snake slid back but then opened its mouth.

"Helen, you are here now. You didn't need to come," said the snake.

"Who are you? I think I am under the influence of something," said Helen.

"You are, and you are not," said the snake.

"What do you want? We are on a mission to save Earth?" said Helen.

"Of course you are. I'm not exactly a friend. But I will be since you are dedicating yourself to stopping the tragic circumstances," said the snake.

"You're just a vision or hallucination. You are somehow just related to the vessel. We know that much and something about the Earth," said Helen.

Jett noticed Helen holding a branch behind her back and looking ready to strike the snake. He moved to the other side of the clearing to have a better view and to get to the snake without attracting too much attention. Jett saw some overhanging tree branches covering the clearing. He began climbing the tree and looked down at Helen, conversing with the snake.

"Yes, but who? What is the solution to the problem now? You need an answer, Helen, and it only lies in the who," said the snake.

"The who?" said Helen.

"You will find whoever is doing this and save millions. You will birth a new world," said the snake.

The ground beneath and around the snake and Helen began to shake. The clearing surrounded by forests shook furiously. The shaking snapped the branches Jett was on, and he landed on his back behind Helen. The snake coiled in retaliation and then jumped at Helen. The snake wrapped itself around Helen. A crackling sound began around Helen, then a disc shaped like a moon appeared, and stars around her body in the shape of a skirt further appeared. Jett ran in the other direction, not looking back until he hid behind a tree.

The mighty snake lifted Helen. And then, Jett raised his hands to his eyes. The glare from the bright light coming from Helen's waist pierced the tree. Jett awoke in the basement, and the strange man still looked at him. He looked around, and Helen was still in a deep trance or unconscious. He shook her. She suddenly jolted up from where she was and screamed.

The strange man continued to look at them until the sound of men was heard from above them, where the doorway to the basement was at the front of the room. The skulls above them flickered with candlelight. Jett looked around where the man was sitting. He found some paper with the image of a Sphinx. There were some more. The strange man cleared his throat to speak.

"You must go to the desert—a vision quest you must go on. Go to Mexico for a spirit guide," said the strange man.

"What's your name again?" Jett asked. He thought it was random of the man to say they should go to Mexico, but he was looking for answers. He looked the man over again.

"Tell them Viento sent you. You'll know who to find because the wind will lead the way," said Viento.

The sounds of people clamoring down the stairs to the basement continued when they reached the door. The door creaks open to reveal Corporal Balco and some military personnel. Jett and Helen simultaneously looked at Corporal Balco and the men, and when they looked back to find Viento, he was gone.

"Oh my god, I'm so glad you're here, Corporal Balco," Helen said.

Jett briefly got jealous of the corporal, as Helen seemed more attuned to him now than she was to him. Some medical personnel were with them, checking both out within a couple of minutes. Jett began giving Corporal Balco information about what they had discovered from Viento and the papers about the room.

"You said some of the papers have the Sphinx emblem on them," said Corporal Balco.

"Yes, sir. It looks exactly like the tattoo the attackers had on them," said Jett.

"What else did this man named Viento say?" said Corporal Balco.

"He said we need to go to Mexico to find a spirit guide," said Jett.

"Spirits? I thought Command had us with you for scientific reasons," said Corporal Balco

"I know. But there is so much more going on than we know about," said Jett.

An alarm suddenly sounded on Corporal Balco's wristbands and the personnel. They looked at their bands and called back to base camp—a look of concern washed over Corporal Balco's face.

"We need to get back to base camp," said Corporal Balco.

"Is it urgent?" said Helen.

"The Anomaly is on the move around New Orleans. It has taken over the southern part of Louisiana quickly and has encircled New Orleans," said Corporal Balco.

"Alright, Helen, we need to get going," commanded Jett.

When they returned to base camp, Jett looked at the sky above New Orleans. A dense fog was coming toward them. Jett looked at all the equipment at base camp and decided to download as much data as possible to his phone and watch. He looked at some of the notes he had downloaded, and some were for him. He decided to scroll through them. His heart sank as he read a tagged note on the computer. His family was dead, including his father. He held onto the desk that was in front of him. He wanted to stop whatever was causing all this pain. Pain like he just felt. A stabbing pain that went beneath his skin and made him want to scream. Some tears rose from inside him, but he tried to repress them.

He crouched and put his face in his hands and cried. He had been hoping beyond hope that his father and family were still alive. He now knew whatever this was, beyond scientific objectivity and hope.

IX

The whirl of the airplane's engines drowned out all the feelings Jett was experiencing from the death of his father and family. He sat at the back and did not want to talk to Helen, Corporal Balco, or anyone. He looked out the window as the plane rose from the tarmac, and the Anomaly continued to roll in, blurring the city out of existence. Jett scrolled through his notes again. Commander and Captain Meno had held up their miasma theory.

Command had been tracking criminal activity and noticed some high-profile crimes in Memphis, Tennessee, and Akron, Ohio. These cities still had not fallen to the Anomaly, the fire, or the orbs. However, there was gang-like activity, with reports of persons with Sphinx tattoos.

Viento had led them in the other direction to Mexico. Jett did not know the correlation, but Viento said the answer would lie somewhere where they were headed. Helen glanced over at Jett with a glare. Jett knew she wanted him near, but he hurt too badly. He felt the pain of his loss in his stomach and chest. It was hard to touch his computer pad.

He took a deep breath as the plane hit a higher altitude. He was staring at the airplane's ceiling when an orange light lit up the cabin. He sat directly up in his chair. The rest of the passengers were sleeping. He opened the blinds of the window and peered out across the sky. The fire was flowing in a billowing way. It was huffing and puffing. It looked like it was about to begin its rampage across the Earth.

He walked to the cockpit and started to pound on the door. Jett could not open it up because of security restrictions. He was about to return to his seat and hope for the best when Corporal Balco woke up and looked out the window. Orange light cascaded on his face. He walked up to Jett.

"Jett, what is going on? Have you heard anything from Command?" said Corporal Balco.

"The fire is back, covering more of Texas," said Jett.

"Have you heard anything from Command?" said Corporal Balco.

"Nothing," said Jett.

The cockpit latch opened, and the pilot appeared. He looked tired and frightened. Some military personnel who were in the cockpit filed out.

"What's going on, captain?" said Corporal Balco.

"We are going as fast as possible to stay ahead of the fire. We will reach El Paso, Texas, in an hour. You guys might as well get some sleep. We are in contact with command back in Houston," said the captain.

Jett looked out the window next to his chair in the cabin. The sun was in the west, adding another menacing glow to the fire. He set his alarm for an hour before they would reach El Paso.

***

The fire had stopped when they reached their base camp in Fort Bliss, next to El Paso. Fort Bliss was taking in civilians and evacuating them. Jett sent some messages to Command on his enclosed email server. Helen went with Corporal Balco to retrieve more materials for the base camp for their run to Mexico. Jett realized they were moving opposite to where people were going across the border. He sent messages to the computers stationed at each evacuee's bedside.

Jett looked up at the big television above the evacuee room as the messages went out to the people. He felt anger rise in his spine as he looked at the image of a tattooed sphinx from their files of the attackers.

Corporal Balco and Helen returned from getting materials and began packing for their move across the border. Jett looked at Helen. She looked more interested in Corporal Balco than in him. Her hair glistened in the desert sun. To the north, Fort Bliss and El Paso, Jett could see a coming dust storm, which was kicked up by the fire from the sky. He sighed as he continued to feel the loss of his family and Peter.

He wanted their lives not to have died in vain. Corporal Balco signaled for Jett and Helen to move to the front of the base camp for pick-up to move to the border.

By the time they moved to the border, the dust storm had rolled in, covering the sky and darkening the sun. So much dust had accumulated inside their noses and shoes in Ciudad Juárez. Jett tussled the dust out of his hair when he was in the bathroom of an empty restaurant. He looked in the mirror and took in the darker tan he had on his face despite the winter months.

When Jett walked out of the bathroom, a man in a black leather jacket was at the doorway. He was flicking open a pocketknife and closing it repeatedly. Corporal Balco had gone down the street to see if anyone was left worth talking to near the border. Jett was leery when he approached the man, but knew he had to ask a few questions.

"Need any help, sir?" asked Jett hesitantly.

"Buenos tardes," said the man.

Jett squirmed a bit. His Spanish was mainly broken, and he wanted to keep his communication plain and straightforward. He stuck out his hand in a greeting. When he did, the man took his hand back and smiled.

"You are not from here?" said the man.

"No, sir, I'm from Houston, Texas, actually," said Jett.

"I'm with Viento. I'm like the wind coming in; once I am here, there's no telling when I'll show up next," said the man.

"Yes, we are because Viento sent us," said Jett.

"So, you know about the vessel, the orbs, the Sphinx organization, etc.," said the man.

"Yes," said Jett.

"I'll take you to Juan Delgado. He has all the information about the Sphinxes. The ones you probably want to get revenge on, hombre," said the man.

"Thanks for referring us; when can we meet with this Juan Delgado?" said Jett.

"Gather your things, and we will meet with him," said the man.

When the man said this, Corporal Balco stepped through the door. He looked the man up and down, then at Jett. Corporal Balco had collected dust samples as some of his equipment hung around his belt.

"You found us some information, Jett! Good job!" said Corporal Balco.

Despite people saying he should learn to take them, Jett did not like receiving compliments. Helen came back from across the street. She had come back with some notes and an old computer pad. She must have gotten it from somewhere.

"So…we are all here," said Jett.

They were taken further into the city and went down and walked among cement walls filled with graffiti. Eventually, they came to a housing section, stepped inside, and found a man standing.

"You are Jett Sanchez, I assume," said the man.

"Yes," said Jett assertively.

"I'm Juan Delgado. We have been expecting you," said Juan. He looked at Corporal Balco and eyed Helen with lust. He walked to her and ran his fingers through her hair.

"You know you can just ask," said Helen flippantly. She caught his hand. Corporal Balco moved her hand away and pushed her back away from Juan.

"None of this man, today. Lives are at stake," said Corporal Balco.

"Alright, I won't ask for the woman. But I need something in return for information about the Sphinxes. Business has taken a hit with all this going on around the world and in the city," said Juan.

"We don't bribe with bad guys. You were just a recommendation from someone we met," said Corporal Balco.

"A bad guy. No. No. No. The Sphinxes are the bad guys. I am just a middleman, nothing more," said Juan.

"You are a middleman, and no one else can ask you anything. Everyone is gone. We need our information now," said Corporal Balco.

"Well, that's a matter of who knows what. Even if I tell you, you may not believe me. This goes high up. This whole cover-up and operation," said Juan.

"So, what can you give us?" said Helen.

"Well, from one drug user to the next—I could give you some ayahuasca. You'll need to go on a vision quest with whatever powers these things have. This battle with these forces will be hard, and it has affected the United States government," said Juan.

"So, you expect us to go on a trip," said Corporal Balco.

"Well, yes. These forces are ancient and surpass normal medical and psychiatric knowledge," said Juan.

"What does this have to do with the Sphinxes?" said Jett curtly.

"The Sphinxes are a criminal organization masquerading as a research organization on the one hand to the United States government and on the other hand operating as a drug cartel and terrorist organization. Some high-level US government officials have been implicated in their attacks, including the US President," said Juan.

Jett did not even scratch his head. Instead, he clenched his hands into a fist and banged his knuckles on the wall. He never admitted how hard Peter's death had hit him until now. A criminal organization killed him—he was now saying it over and over in his mind.

"What do you think their motives are?" Corporal Balco scoffed. He adjusted his equipment and gun, showing his discomfort with the topic. Juan raised his hands in defense.

"Hey, no hard feelings, man; I know you work for them. It seems they want these forces—the fire, the orbs, the Anomaly—to destroy the world or at least take it over completely. I would not trust anyone," said Juan informatively.

"Even though you are telling us not to trust anyone, I think you know more than you are saying," said Corporal Balco as he quickly raised his gun to Juan's head.

"Hey, hey, hey, Corporal Balco, hold on there! Juan is trying to help us there," said Jett.

"How far is this going?" said Corporal Balco, brow furrowed in rage.

"They want to drug people. They have some augmented substances from somewhere. Not from Earth. I am unsure about the substance's relation to the orbs and everything. The criminal masterminds want to release it into the water supply of major cities," said Juan.

"Son of a—" said Corporal Balco.

"How do we prevent all this from happening?" said Helen.

"You need to keep what you are doing. You have made it this far. Whatever it is you are doing, it's working. You were not supposed to have found me or Viento," said Juan.

"Do you have a name on our main guy—the guy who killed my friend, Peter?" said Jett.

"His name is William Sono…He was supposedly one of their first recruits after their founder, Patrick Suther, picked him up from the streets of your hometown of Houston," said Juan.

They swarmed past the restaurant's windows. The fire howled, and the silent, orange glow of the fire in the sky lit the restaurant inside, where they were standing. Juan looked up and flipped over a phone.

While Juan was dialing on his phone, Jett noticed a tattoo of snakes on Juan's hands. He thought about New Orleans, Viento, and the vision or hallucination they saw of the snake. Jett thought about his hunches. He did not feel like a scientist. He felt more like a minion of politicians and a shaman interpreting animal entrails.

"Who are you dialing?" said Jett.

"A friend. You guys will be impressed by who he is. He's the best Mexico has to offer in this fight. Well, at least in this city," said Juan.

Jett thought about the snake's words and how they were meant just for Helen. He, Helen, and Corporal Balco were on edge enough to consider someone's tattoos in their decisions. They needed all the help they could get in this plan to save the world.

"So, who is he?" said Jett.

"Dr. Martin Soliz," said Juan Delgado.

"A doctor of what?" said Helen.

"He's a brilliant man. No worries. He has a doctorate in anthropology, archaeology, and history. And, some others like biology and physics," said Juan.

"We do not need any more help," said Corporal Balco.

Jett held up his hand to Corporal Balco in a sign for him to calm down so they could talk to Juan Delgado. Corporal Balco glared at Jett, and the look caught Jett off guard. This was the first time Jett questioned the loyalty of those given to him by Command, and had Corporal Balco since exposure, since Juan implicated the US government and officials.

"So, what do you say? Want to join a team, Juan? said Jett.

"I need to hear back from Dr. Soliz. But, yes, I would like to take you up on your offer," said Juan.

Jett looked over at Helen, who looked slightly irritated. He grabbed her arm and pulled her aside next to the restaurant bar. He looked into her vibrant eyes. The wind clamored at the restaurant's roof. There was not much they could do as the dust storm continued and the fire in the sky approached.

"Helen, we need him," said Jett.

"I know. It doesn't feel right, though. He seems like a potential enemy. He could kill, you know. I don't want to lose you," said Helen.

"I'll keep an eye on him and tell Corporal Balco to do the same," said Jett.

Jett let Helen stay at the bar and went to where Juan and Corporal Balco were. While walking up, Juan was still on the phone, abruptly ending the call. Jett had brought his computer pad with him. He looked up at the sky. They needed to leave now for the cleanest escape possible.

"So, what is the news?" said Corporal Balco.

"Alright, I have Dr. Soliz on board. He'll meet us here at the restaurant. We will take him to Fort Bliss," said Juan.

"Does he know the current situation?" said Corporal Balco.

Juan looked out over the sky. The fire in the sky had turned to a saffron color. Electrical lines flickered everywhere with bright, white light. Some Mexican civilians were taking shelter in a building across the street.

Jett made some calculations about the fire on his computer pad. He squinted, and then his heart skipped a beat. The information from Command showed they were in for it. The fire had been confirmed to have a cycle when it expanded, and orbs suddenly appeared. Jett was about to tell Corporal Balco when he heard screaming.

Jett did not think twice about entering the streets filled with the heavy winds of a potential alien encounter. People were running, and he brought his hand up to his brow to block the glow from the fire in the sky. He squinted.

Orbs were beginning to appear from the fire in the sky and come out of nowhere. Some blue orbs were coming from the ground. More people began to run, and Jett went to where they were running. A handful of the orbs had taken victims. Some people were frozen in place by the blue orbs. Another group of orange orbs danced above the houses and buildings of the city. Some of the motionless and turned-off cars began to turn on, and Jett briefly thought the orange orbs were playing with him.

That was until they began to follow the people running the streets, hovering over them, grabbing them, and throwing them to the ground. Jett ran back to the restaurant, and Juan, Corporal Balco, and Helen stared at him.

"Where were you?" said Helen.

"I got some information from Command. We need to move now. We are in for it. Where is Dr. Soliz?" said Jett.

"He is about five minutes away, coming down the main road," said Juan.

"Alright, when he arrives, let's ready ourselves to encounter anything and everything," said Jett.

X

Dr. Soliz was a large, rotund man with square black glasses. He carried a briefcase and a computer pad with a scanner. Before he shook Jett, Helen, and Corporal Balco's hands, he scanned everything around them and their bodies.

He looked up at the sky, which had a thin line of darkness in the west compared to the glowing fire in the sky. More people were running in the streets with belongings, children, and pets. The sky was ripped with white lightning, and the fire in the sky roared.

"We have to get back to Fort Bliss," said Dr. Soliz.

Corporal Balco looked at one of his computer screens and read. The fire in the sky—which the Mexicans had named El Diablo—was moving fast, but not fast enough that they could not outrun it. Jett summarized that they had gotten what they had come for and did the best they could for the people of the area and both countries, the US and Mexico.

Jett and everyone else boarded an old truck and headed to the border. When they returned to Fort Bliss, the fire had stalled, but its roar persisted. Jett and Helen went with Corporal Balco, Juan Delgado, and Dr. Soliz. Dr. Soliz scrambled to the science stations of the Command Center. Soliz input some data via his phone and started calculating on a dry-erase board. Juan Delgado sat and ate an avocado. He didn't seem enamored with what Dr. Soliz was doing as he peered around Command.

"There's nothing to this," said Delgado.

Dr. Soliz had hardly spoken since arriving. He seemed to be in some distant land, far removed from what was happening. Jett observed that his calculations were making sense as he sat and looked at the fire in the sky, El Diablo. El Diablo was so close that he started to perspire. Some of the military personnel were evacuating and taking equipment with them.

Helen had remained dutiful to her purpose as a team member. Captain Meno would be proud. She continued to catalog everyone's reactions to their environment: their moods, behaviors, diet, etc. Occasionally switching papers and notes with Corporal Balco, Helen had not interacted with Jett much. Jett took this as a good thing. Their lives had been on the line. When he was looking out the window, he saw what looked like a local family. They were huddled against the wall of the Command building. Jett did not know how they had gotten so close to Command. They were frightened.

Jett grabbed some masks, blankets, and rations and went outside to the family. The father covered the mother and daughter from the dust and winds. Jett beckoned them to come over and take some shelter from the situation.

"Over here," he shouted at the man.

The man gave him a thumbs-up, grabbed his daughter and wife, and ran towards Jett. The winds had picked up, and debris and other items were beginning to gather around Command. Jett found a lieutenant and ensured he would find safety for the family. The family smiled through their horror-stricken faces.

"Thank you," said the father.

Corporal Balco saw what Jett had done and walked over to where Jett was. He placed his hand on his shoulder and momentarily talked to the lieutenant about the orders for the family. Helen saw all this as well and shot Jett a smile.

"That was a decent thing you did there," said Corporal Balco.

"Thanks, you haven't done too badly yourself," said Jett with sincerity.

"The next thing you know, I'll be getting a promotion," said Corporal Balco.

The two of them fist-pumped. Annoyed by the situation, Delgado coughed into his hands and kept coughing. Dr. Soliz had gone over to a table and was at a computer. The winds swept through the Command room and scattered some of Dr. Soliz's papers. The family exiting the room was thrown aside, held only by the lieutenant. Corporal Balco ran to shut the door of Command with the help of some other soldiers and Jett.

"We need to leave," said Dr. Soliz.

"No, really," said Delgado, now picking up some peanut shells.

Dr. Soliz did not take Delgado's sarcasm and quickly got up and approached him. Delgado tossed his peanuts to the ground and stood up to Dr. Soliz. Helen was watching the entire thing.

"No, guys don't. We don't need any of this kind of trouble," said Helen.

"If it weren't for you and your type, we wouldn't be in this situation," said Dr. Soliz.

"My type? Oh, you mean the rest of the garbage of Mexico," said Delgado.

"You know what I mean," said Dr. Soliz, clenching his fists.

"Hey, guys, hey," said Corporal Balco, separating them.

"The doctor seems to have a problem with me," said Delgado.

"None more than usual," said Dr. Soliz.

The light fixtures of the Command room began to shake, followed by everything around them. The daughter and mother screamed as some beams from the ceiling in an adjacent room fell. Jett and Helen went under a table for cover.

As soon as they did, the room stopped shaking. Jett ran over to the window and looked up into El Diablo. The fire's roar was deafening, and Jett knew they had little time.

"We need to head north," said Jett.

"Hold on," said Corporal Balco.

"What do you mean? I'm in command. You're just a corporal, Corporal Balco," said Jett.

"We work together. We need to consult with Dr. Soliz," said Corporal Balco.

"Do you have anything yet, Dr. Soliz?" said Corporal Balco.

"If you wanted to head up north, the forces in power are on your side. I found evidence that some of the glyphic writing is related to the petroglyphs you can find in New Mexico," said Dr. Soliz.

"What does that have to do with anything? Where will that take us?" said Jett.

"The petroglyphs have experienced some seismic disturbances in their area, like we just had," said Dr. Soliz.

"Can you be clearer, Doctor?" said Helen.

"Yes, the samples you took from the ship have been cross-analyzed with samples from the petroglyphs. The dates are relatively recent in geologic and historical records. The alien samples date from about 800 to 600 years ago. Right before the Spanish contact with the Americas," said Dr. Soliz.

"So, that alien ship—or whatever—was here before we were here, the Westerners," said Corporal Balco.

"Yes, precisely," said Dr. Soliz.

"So, what do we need to do exactly?" inquired Jett.

"We need to get to the petroglyphs simply before El Diablo, the Anomaly, the orbs, or anything else gets to them. I've noticed a pattern with all this alien activity, and the pattern is global. The sites in New Mexico will lead us to our next opportunity to prevent disaster or communicate with whatever this is," said Dr. Soliz.

"We need to get Command on the phone. Helen, set up an area to take a call. And Dr. Soliz, how much time could we have?" said Jett.

"Perhaps half a day, given the pattern," said Dr. Soliz.

Jett turned around to face the family, crouched against a wall again with a lieutenant next to them. The little girl and her mother were covering their eyes. El Diablo's roar and brightness were unrelenting.

"Lieutenant, what's your name?" said Jett.

"Lieutenant Radisson, sir," said the lieutenant.

"Get this family some food and water," said Jett further.

"It should be noted, sir, that there may be no other place for this family to go. The last of the personnel from the base has evacuated," said Radisson.

"So, you're with us," said Jett.

The family got up from crouching and headed toward the back of the room with Radisson. The earth shook again, and El Diablo's roar went throughout the area. The little girl looked up at Jett.

"Thank you," she said.

"No problem. What is your name?" said Jett.

"Maria Herrera," she said quietly.

"Well, I'm sure you will be safe here. We will be heading north to New Mexico, where all this bad stuff can't get to us," said Jett.

Maria clung to his leg, and Jett smiled at her mother and father. He didn't mind her clinging, but needed to finish his work. She finally gave him one big hug on the leg, took a step back, and looked up at him.

"Mommy and Daddy, this man is going to protect us. I know it," said Maria.

Helen was watching Jett and the family, and she came over and placed her hand on Maria's hand. Helen smiled comfortingly and looked at Jett with those clever, beautiful eyes. Jett knew Helen was proud of him and that they had done their best to fulfill the mission given to them.

"We need you, Maria," said her mother.

"We're going to get them in a jeep. You are all coming with us, right?" said Lieutenant Radisson.

"Yes, sir," said Dr. Soliz.

I was looking Dr. Soliz up and down for a while. Delgado was sure an unfriendly man, Jett thought, given the circumstances. Corporal Balco started to help Dr. Soliz gather up his things. Helen did, too. Jett went over to Delgado.

"You need to calm down, you know. Getting angry isn't going to solve anything. Did you know Dr. Soliz before everyone met?" said Jett.

"Maybe I knew him. He knows we are in the right for doing what we do—for what we did and continue to do," said Delgado.

Jett squinted. He didn't know precisely what Delgado was talking about, but Delgado spoke stubbornly. He continued to munch on peanuts, which Jett thought was weird. He went over to a cooler and found some rations. He gave some to Delgado. Delgado scoffed at them.

"I used to eat like a king in Mexico. That is food not even meant for dogs," said Delgado.

"Alright, you don't want it. We need to cooperate. Everything is on the line with us, " said Jett.

Jett thought about everyone back at Command in Galveston. He felt him growing nervous about his mission, like never before. Cooperation wasn't a strong suit of what they did back in the day. It was more of a have-to situation and a duty. Now, other people's lives were at stake. There was a secretive air about Delgado that Jett couldn't place.

"Dr. Soliz, we will put all your equipment and papers in the back of a jeep," said Corporal Balco.

"Wherever everything I've done goes, I go," he said affirmatively.

By the time darkness came, they were ready. Jett did not like that they were traveling at night, but the personnel were well equipped, and El Diablo lit up the sky with its orange, red, and yellow hues. They rolled out from Fort Bliss at about 11 a.m.

A streak of saffron-colored what looked like heated gas rumbled across the sky. That was the thing with the fire and the other forces they had encountered. They looked otherworldly for the most part and were only described when they seemed to come into this world. Maybe they were not in any real danger yet, and they couldn't see this battle, though Jett.

Although the Anomaly, El Diablo, and the orbs had already taken lives, people and countries worldwide fought back and took steps against their seemingly inevitable destruction. Jett and Helen sat in the middle of the Jeep with Corporal Balco, Delagado, and Dr. Soliz. Lieutenant Radisson was in another Jeep with Maria and her mother and father.

They sped up the highway into New Mexico. As soon as they reached Las Cruces, the nearby mountains sheltered them from El Diablo. Jett did some calculations by looking at a map and directed the soldier driving the Jeep to the petroglyph site north of Las Cruces. It was the Three Rivers Petroglyph site. Dr. Soliz exited his site, sticking his head and body out of the sunroof. He had night-vision goggles on, and Dr. Soliz looked into the darkness.

"Yes, it's happening like I predicted," said Dr. Soliz.

A glow came from the site in the distance. Jett had never been to Alaska, where the aurora borealis could be seen, but he imagined that it would look like that, only closer to the ground. Both Jeeps pulled up just outside the site. Some of the soldiers from Radisson's jeep got out and took some readings with full protective gear on. The glow was sometimes more intense than El Diablo. The soldiers determined it was not harsh enough to wear protective eyewear. More of Dr. Soliz's equipment was unpacked from the army jeeps. Here, they would stand against everything humankind had encountered so far.

"Dr. Soliz, we need your passcode to set up some of these stations and equipment," said Radisson.

"Yes, it's GammaEcho350," said Dr. Soliz.

Jett went up to a boulder and stood on it. He brought some binoculars, which made him feel old. He remembered binoculars when he and his dad went camping. The glow and lights from the petroglyphs did not seem to move in any discernible pattern to Jett. Yet the clouds were hanging low, which was odd for this area and time of year, but it was weather after all. Helen was taking notes about some of the petroglyphs she could see with her flashlight. Nothing had changed.

"I'll wait until morning to take further notes and samples. Do you think these things are more like crop circles now that all this is happening?" said Helen.

"It sure seems like it," said Jett.

A harsh wind began to pick up, coming from the deepest part of the site and fanning out, and sandblasted Jett and Helen. They ran back into the jeep and could hear Maria crying in the jeep next to them. The wind was whipping so hard that Dr. Soliz, Lieutenant Radisson, and others tied a rope to themselves and the jeep. Delgado was watching this in an amused way. Jett looked at Helen as Delgado laughed.

"You know you can stop laughing," said Jett.

"I laugh when I want and at what I want. How could you not laugh? This guy had it coming to him," said Delgado.

The wind suddenly lessened, and the air sat still while the dancing lights over the petroglyph site continued. Dr. Soliz ran over to some of his equipment and began to mutter loudly. Jett saw this, got out of the jeep, and approached Dr. Soliz.

"No, no, no, this can't be happening," said Dr. Soliz.

"What, what is it?" said Jett.

"El Diablo is changing course to us, but it looks like it can't strike everywhere," said Dr. Soliz.

"So, where does that leave us?"

"We need to move further north to Albuquerque and northern New Mexico," said Dr. Soliz.

"But we just got here," informed Jett in an irritated tone.

"You don't want to die, do you?" said Dr. Soliz.

Jett looked at Corporal Balco, Lieutenant Radisson, and the work of other soldiers and personnel. Dr. Soliz's words hit Jett, so he ran up to Corporal Balco and started using the scanner on one of the pieces of equipment.

"I decided to join your work," said Jett.

"Sounds like a plan," said Corporal Balco while looking back at Dr. Soliz.

XI

When the day arrived, the lights above the petroglyph site were gone, although the air around the site felt unsettling. Jett moved a little in the middle seat of the jeep. A blanket was over him, separating him from the cool night of the desert. Helen was resting her head on his leg, which he enjoyed. This mission to save the world had grown distant, and he craved something more tangible.

Corporal Balco had slept outside with some other soldiers. Jett smelled the crisp bacon and beans someone was cooking. He gently moved Helen onto the elongated seat. He lightly got out of the jeep and stood before the petroglyph site. In the desert, there was not much movement. It was still. This wrecked Jett's nerves, and the knot grew in his stomach. All this devastation and lives lost, and they have yet to figure out what indeed has happened, what caused all this, and other answers to questions. Some mesquite rustled nearby Jett.

He drew his gun, but then he heard a squeal from the mesquite bushes. As Jett was looking, a female coyote and her young emerged. The mother was nursing a can of beans for her young. Somehow, Jett thought life would be preserved if humanity were not. Jett thought this was overly optimistic, but he knew he must stay optimistic for survival reasons.

Lieutenant Radisson and the family awoke in the other jeep, and the coyote and her young quickly ran off to find shelter elsewhere in the desert. Dr. Soliz was already doing scans and sending soldiers to take samples of nearby petroglyphs. Some soldiers even took etchings of the petroglyphs despite the risk of damage.

"I see you awake," said a voice.

Jett turned around. It was Delgado. The older Mexican was already eating a can of beans. He had a phone and some antiquated walkie-talkies with him.

"Where did you get those pieces of technology?" inquired Jett about the walkie-talkies.

"I kept it on me to keep in contact with my clientele," said Delgado.

Jett's brow furrowed. He did not like that response. This was a crisis, and Delgado still acted like business was as usual. The fight between Delgado and Dr. Soliz crossed his mind. Moreover, Jett remembered another target they were after: the Sphinxes. The cataclysmic arrival of El Diablo caused everyone to forget about some supposed plot. Jett summed it all up as a conspiracy. Delgado was looking at Jett with a grin.

"You think I was lying, don't you, about the Sphinxes?" said Delgado.

"No, I think we have not found proof yet of drugs or malice or conspiracy," said Jett.

"Think again," said Delgado as he pointed past Jett to some soldiers.

The soldiers were carrying what looked like rice bags on the outside, but they had been cutting them open as well. They had placed the bags downwind, and they were wearing gas masks. Some other soldiers quickly handed out masks to Dr. Soliz and the family. To Jett's surprise, Helen was already in a mask. Fairly soon, everyone was, including Jett.

"Looks like we didn't escape anything," said Jett.

"Well, we are away from El Diablo and everything," said Helen.

The two of them went to Dr. Soliz and Corporal Balco's station. They were exchanging words that Jett could overhear as he approached. Maria's mother covered her ears. Jett briefly thought that he should get Maria's parents' names.

"Dr. Soliz, you're not helping," said Corporal Balco.

"We need to find the sources of these drugs. They are more powerful than peyote and ayahuasca and more attuned to the human body and mind," said Dr. Soliz.

"Juan Delgado thinks it's the Sphinxes," said Corporal Balco.

"I think the answer to the Sphinxes could be right under our noses. We need to move fast. We are ahead of El Diablo, but there is still the anomaly and the orbs," said Dr. Soliz.

"Delgado, we need you at the chemistry station," said Corporal Balco.

A soldier who was at the biological station screamed and clutched his hand at the same time. This came out of the corner of Jett's eye. It was quick enough that Jett second-guessed himself and hesitated. Soon enough, the soldier's hand had melted off his arm.

"I thought these were only samples," said Lieutenant Radisson to Corporal Balco.

"They were until now," said Corporal Balco.

Some personnel began to attend to the wounded soldier, and Jett was going over there to help when he felt a jolt of pain go through his body. He stood staring out into the desert across the petroglyph site. His eyes felt like being pulled open, as if compelled to look at something. A hazy fog began to appear on the site.

"Oh, no!" said Jett.

A thin, scattered line of light appeared in the sky and went into the ground. When it hit, several boulders split open. Debris flew onto and past the encampments and jeeps. A soupy haze spewed forth from the scattered line. Jett knew what it was. It was the Anomaly, and it had come to them.

His eyes stared into the haziness. The gaseous fog seeped through the line in the sky and spilled over some boulders. Some jackrabbits hopped out of the way of the mist only to be consumed by it. This time, the Anomaly did not seem to be freezing or killing everything it encountered. It was devouring.

Several soldiers brought some explosive weapons and fired them at the Anomaly. It did nothing. The haze seemed to grow and feed on the agitation produced by the explosions. Jett felt the pain in his body, and it was paralyzing. He could see the monstrous cloud heading toward him, and Jett knew that his time may be up, but not just yet. He felt a tug on his shirt that pulled him around. It was Helen.

She pulled Jett towards the Jeeps, where the family and others crouched. This wouldn't do any good, he thought. They were done for. Delgado had not budged at all. He stood laughing as Dr. Soliz and the others struggled to run away. Dr Soliz was holding something in his hands that he gave to Lieutenant Radisson.

"Fire it at the Anomaly," said Dr. Soliz.

Lieutenant Radisson turned to a firing position and let the device rip into the Anomaly. Jet was astounded. The Anomaly seemed to retreat every time Lieutenant Radisson struck it with the device. Delgado approached Lieutenant Radisson and gestured to rip it out of his hands. That was the wrong move by Delgado. Corporal Balco was on top of him in no time. The Anomaly retreated to its original position in the sky, along the light line.

"What do you do that for?" screamed Corporal Balco at Delgado.

It's no use fighting. All you will do is alert the Sphinxes and the forces behind the destruction," said Delgado.

"This man is officially a saboteur," said Dr. Soliz. "he should be punished."

Jett got up and walked towards them. It was his time to lead. He needed to take control of this situation. Delgaldo dealt with it, and then Corporal Balco took over.

"Delgado," said Jett, "We'll deal with you after all this is done. In the meantime, I'll message Command about your actions."

Delgado huffed.

"It's no use, Jett; the Sphinxes already know we're here." Dr. Soliz used some of their technology and the frequency it is on to neutralize the Anomaly," said Delgado.

"What frequency is he talking about, Dr. Soliz?" said Helen.

"It's the frequency from some other universe, where, I believe, these forces originate, and where the vessel in Galveston is also from," said Dr. Soliz.

"Will the Sphinxes or others find out we used it?" said Jett.

I was perfecting the technology when the Anomaly arrived, so there's no telling. " It was only a prototype," Dr. Soliz said.

The Anomaly was still in the sky. Its green hue was accompanied by the characteristic saffron and ochre colors that Jett had seen in so many instances of these forces. Jett looked over at Dr. Soliz's equipment, which had some damage.

"We need to notify Command what has happened," said Jett.

"I'll message them," said Lieutenant Radisson.

The chaos unleashed in the otherwise peaceful desert setting was felt everywhere. Mesquite bushes and tumbleweeds were burning, and flocks of birds were dead or dying near where the Anomaly had stopped.

That is what was needed: quiet and solitude. Jett returned to work with the others on Dr. Soliz's stations. Jett had something to attend to before returning to work. He returned to the rear of the other jeep to find the family. They were still there.

"Hey, how are you holding up?" said Jett to them.

"You said you would protect us," Maria said.

"What kind of monsters are coming?" the father asked.

"Are they divine or punishment from God?" said the mother.

"Nothing of the sort," said Jett.

"I'm sorry, but I did not catch your names," said Jett, looking at the parents.

"I'm Hector, and this is my wife, Carmen," said Hector.

"Nice to meet you," said Jett.

"So, will any of this go away? When can we go back to our homes?" said Carmen.

"We don't know yet. This may sound far-fetched, but we need to save the world. We believe that the world could end because of what is happening, or at least the world as we know it," said Jett.

Jett was preoccupied talking to Hector and his family when he noticed dust in the distance. Not again, thought Jett. He ran over and grabbed some old binoculars. He peered through them, and instead of another strike by the Anomaly, an armored truck was revealed.

"We've got company, everyone!" he shouted to Corporal Balco and the others.

Lieutenant Radisson ran over to him and ordered some soldiers to arm themselves and, if necessary, take out the vehicle with their weapons. Jett was walking over to Dr. Soliz when the armored vehicle abruptly fired at the Anomaly. The Anomaly somehow started to grow again and swallowed a soldier out in the desert. Dr. Soliz began to gather his belongings and shouted at Delgado.

"I knew you were a backstabber," said Dr. Soliz to Delgado.

"You want to rule the world now, everyone, but we have better ideas," said Delgado.

Delgado was holding a gun, which he brought out across his chest as protection. Corporal Balco looked at Delgado in disbelief. Corporal Balco went up and stood beside Delgado.

"Don't betray us, Delgado," said Corporal Balco.

You've done some good, Delgado. And you could do more," said Jett.

"Well, I don't intend to," said Delgado.

And, with that, he pressed a button on a device that resembled a tiny cell phone. A blue shield rose over Delgado, and he turned and headed towards the armored truck, which had now stopped about a hundred feet from where they were. By this time, the soldiers were opening fire on the armored truck. They had not taken them out yet. The armored truck was still emitting pulsating energy waves to the Anomaly. And it seemed to become gaseous and grow again.

"We need to book it," said Jett to Corporal Balco.

Helen was gathering the soldiers and equipment away from the onslaught of the Anomaly again. Dr. Soliz was standing alone, looking at the Anomaly with an explosive gun pointing towards the other vehicle. Jett ran up to him to stop any rash action.

"Dr. Soliz, please stop. We need you. " Get in the jeep, and we can leave," Jett said over the nearby explosions.

"It's over, Jet. It's the Sphinxes," said Dr. Soliz.

"No, it isn't," said Jet.

"Or so," said Dr. Soliz as he pointed past Jett towards the desert, a little past the armored truck.

A man stood next to Delgado. He was taller than Jett and had a decent build. His hair was black, and his skin was a creamy white. He appeared to be of mixed race, possibly Asian and Hispanic descent.

"That's William Sono, Jett. The man who killed Peter," said Dr. Soliz.

Heat ran up Jett's spine. He could feel the flush of anger as he clenched his fists. Revenge was staring right before Jett. He was ready. He felt it.

Jett started to run towards Sono, and then he was thrown to the ground. Jett massaged his head. It was throbbing with pain; he thought an explosive had hit him, and he was injured. He sat up and looked before him, only to find Sono standing several feet from him.

"You are a true friend at heart," said Sono.

Jett thought about Sono's words. He didn't have time for self-deprecating humor. He wanted revenge on Peter.

"Peter would be proud," said Sono.

"Why did you kill him? " What do your people want with the world, and why are you doing this?" Jett asked.

"I killed him out of necessity, nothing more. He was in my way. Peter was a tricky one," said Sono.

"He was a good person; he was my best friend," said Peter.

Jett pushed himself up and brushed the desert sand off himself. Jett was through with talking to Sono. He grabbed his weapon and began to target him.

"Stop, Jett," said Helen as she ran beside him.

"What do you mean?" said Jett.

"We need Sono. "We need him to collect information about what's happening," Helen said.

"Can't you see, Helen? " They have attacked us," Jett said.

"I know. But keep your revenge to yourself for now. " Do it for the mission," Helen said.

He could not believe what Helen had just said. Keeping it to himself was not an option. Sono was in his sights when Jett screamed in pain. Helen screamed and fell back away from him. He landed face-first into the dirt and sand of the desert.

There was a taser now on Jett's side. Sono was now inches from him, and he could see his feet. Rolling himself over, Jett saw the face of Delgado with a taser gun. Jett realized that the taser had hit the sling of his rifle on his back. Delgado had just tasered him and betrayed Jett.

"You shouldn't have done that," said Jett.

The Anomaly grew several feet from where Delgado, Sono, and Jett were. Jett's face was flushed with rage. He could feel it. Jett put his foot in the sand and kicked some dirt into Delgado's face.

Rolling away from Sono, Jett pushed Delgado into the Anomaly, automatically consuming him. Jett saw Helen and motioned for her to grab Delgado's taser. She needed to stun Sono.

"Taser Sono!" he screamed.

The Sphinxes in the armored truck had not stopped firing on the soldiers from Jett's side. They were distracted, though. Jett approached the armored truck and climbed onto its top, where the device that opened and closed the Anomaly was stationed. The device was still operational, so Jett opened fire on the Anomaly, halting it in its tracks.

XII

Seeing that Jett was on top of the armored truck. Sono's soldiers had noticed him and turned their weapons on him. Jett did not blink. He turned the Anomaly device on the Sono's soldiers and fired. It vaporized them instantly.

The Anomaly had kicked up dust, and Helen was aiming the taser at Sono. She felt conflicted that Sono was still a key to the puzzle. They could take him in, and he could lead them where they needed to go. And, with that thought, she fired the taser. Sono immediately hit the ground.

Sand and dust were everywhere. Jett felt his anger again. He wanted to kill Sono, but he knew he had to keep him alive because of the mission.

"Jett, don't do anything. " We need to get out of here," Helen said.

"I know. But I want to rid the world of that guy. Peter would want that," said Jett.

"I don't think Peter would want you to take revenge. I think he would want you to remain alive and complete the mission," said Helen.

Corporal Balco and Lieutenant Radisson approached Helen and Sono, and they were arrested. Sono began resisting Corporal Balco and Lieutenant Radisson, and the two soldiers increased their pressure on him. Some of the other soldiers came to relieve Corporal Balco of arresting Sono.

"We need to get out of here, Corporal Balco," said Jett.

"There's an old airport outside of Las Cruces where there are some military planes we could take," said Corporal Balco.

"I think we should go to the airport," said Helen.

"I agree," said Corporal Balco.

The scene in the desert was chaotic. The sand and dirt had been blackened from all the explosions, and some mesquite bushes were on fire. Jett and some other soldiers began collecting some of Dr. Soliz's things. Dr. Soliz was gathering his things and still collecting them by scanning the Anomaly.

"You never give up, Dr. Soliz," said Jett.

"Never," Dr. Soliz said.

"We are heading to an old local airport to get out of here," said Jett.

"Very well. I don't know what good it will do, though. I have reviewed reports of the Anomaly, El Diablo, and the orbs have further appeared across the globe, " said Dr. Soliz.

"We will be heading to wherever the next fight is," said Jett to Dr. Soliz.

"We will need to message Command and inform them of our current location, then obtain the necessary information to determine our next steps," said Helen.

They packed everything and set out for the airport with Sono under custody. The airport was west of Las Cruces, and they radioed to any military aircraft or personnel in the area where they were arriving. Jett and the team scanned radio frequencies for any messages, but none were received.

"Nobody is out there," said Corporal Balco.

"We'll see once we get to the airport," said Jett.

It was deserted when they arrived at the airport, despite reports that it was a military holdout by the US Air Force and Army. Several soldiers and Lieutenant Radisson got out to scope out the area.

"Nobody is here," said Lieutenant Radisson.

"Any word from Command?" said Helen.

Jett heard some whimpers and crying, and he had forgotten about Maria and her family. They were in the backseat, looking as frightened as a beaten dog. Jett walked over to the Jeep and got inside.

"It's okay," said Jett.

"It's not. You guys don't know what you are doing and are going to get us killed," said Hector, the father.

"Hush, Hector, they know. "They are doing their best," Carmen said, wiping away tears. Her consoling words were brushed aside as she turned to her husband, who was cursing the names of Corporal Balco and the rest of the team.

"We will investigate all the planes here. And if we find one fit to fly, we will take it," said Jett.

"Where will you go? Those things are everywhere," said Hector.

"We haven't heard back from Command, but we will go wherever we need to go," said Jett.

"Jett, over here," Helen called out.

"Got to go. "I'll see you all in a bit," Jett said.

Helen was standing by an extensive Air Force Cargo plane. Corporal Balco was in the cockpit. Jett looked over their faces. They looked concerned, and a sense of desperation was in the air.

This plane appears to be safe to take. This plane has all the bells and whistles. It's even long-distance; it can go almost worldwide without refueling. Everyone looks like they just left here in a panic," said Corporal Balco.

"That's understandable. We can start loading everything onto the plane right away," said Helen.

"Where are we off to next?" Jett asked.

"We'll ask Dr. Soliz for a conversation, but he said something about Egypt," said Corporal Balco.

'Egypt? " Have we heard anything from Command?" Jett asked.

"We have only had one dispatch, an old one from Command. It stated that they would continue with your orders and message you again when needed," said Helen.

Hours passed as they readied the plane and filled it with everything necessary for the mission and their survival. Dr. Soliz had calculated that the Anomaly had occurred due to recent fluctuations in the Earth's magnetic field. Jett had informed Dr. Soliz of his hallucinations when interacting with the vessel back in Houston and New Orleans. Despite Jett's certainty and adamance, Dr. Soliz did not accept his belief or argument that these were interconnected.

The day arrived, and the plane took off to the east. Lieutenant Radisson had a pilot's license with the military, and he plotted a course with Dr. Soliz that avoided the areas where the Anomaly and the orbs had appeared on Command maps. A few soldiers fell ill due to some turbulence that Helen had to manage during the flight. There was not much space, so Jett found himself face-to-face with Sono.

"You're fighting a losing war, Jett," said Sono during the flight.

Jett stared straight past him. He did not have time for Sono's talk. The mission would succeed despite the setbacks and obstacles they had faced.

"I think your girl, Helen, is pretty," said Sono.

Jett sighed. Ten hours into the flight, he was still dealing with Sono. Dinner rations were being passed around. Some reached Jett. Turbulence suddenly struck, and the rations flew towards Sono. Sono slammed his handcuffed hands down on the rations. He looked at Jett with a look that only a true deviant does.

"You are going to have to fight me for this," said Sono.

Jett laughed.

"Fight you? I won't fight you. You are as good as dead right now. I could have thrown you off the plane," said Jett.

Well, that comment left a lasting impression. I did not expect such sociopathy from someone like you, Jett," Sono said.

When they were over Europe, Jett gained a window seat and looked out the small, oval window. Jett could see El Diablo stretch for miles over what he assumed were significant cities. Lieutenant Radisson finally alerted everyone on the plane that they were approaching Egypt and about to land. They would land at Cairo International Airport in the desert.

The Cairo airport was like any other, but Dr. Soliz said it looked like the Anomaly had passed by, killing everyone in its wake. He knew because a residue was left behind throughout the airport. Jett looked up at the sky once he was safely inside the airport. The roar of El Diablo was everywhere. Jett missed the peace before all of this happened.

Dr. Soliz happened to pass by, and Jett raised his arms to greet him, shouting. Dr. Soliz was holding a scanner. He looked irritated, though, at Jett's loudness. Jett figured they were headed to the Giza pyramids or other ancient sites, but he felt it was best to check with Dr. Soliz.

"Dr. Soliz, are we headed to the pyramids or somewhere else?" said Jett.

"You got that right. This is an opportunity. Scientists, engineers, and all learned men have wondered about the pyramids. No, we seem to have started to unravel some of their mystery," said Dr. Soliz.

"Like how so?" said Jett.

"Whatever the Sphinxes have done to exacerbate this situation with the forces at their disposal. They seem to have opened portals at significant archaeological sites and cultural centers worldwide," said Dr. Soliz.

Jett heard Dr. Soliz's words loud and clear. They needed to go to the Pyramids, set up camp, and observe any further movements to see if the Sphinxes would interfere again. He noticed a grayish substance that Dr. Soliz was carrying.

"What is that?" said Jett.

"Oh, it's one of the drugs Delgado was dealing. I stole it from him. " He never knew I had it," Dr. Soliz said.

Jett raised an eyebrow.

You don't have to worry about me betraying you, Jett. I was never on Delgado's side nor the Sphinxes. I was more trapped than anything," Dr. Soliz said.

"What do you need us to do once we arrive at the pyramids?" Jett asked.

"We need not meet the Sphinxes; that is what we need. And, to complete our mission," Dr. Soliz said.

Jett looked up at the blackened sun, which had risen high in the sky over the Pyramids and the Saharan Desert. The sun looked like it burned from its core, and blackness itched across it from El Diablo.

They had managed to get to the Pyramids without incident. They began to analyze the area and searched for reports of the Anomaly or the orbs. Within hours of reaching the Pyramids, reports from Egypt's Mediterranean coast surfaced that the Anomaly had appeared. Orbs also began to dance above the sky of Cairo, wielding destruction. Dr. Soliz, this time, had a solution. He wanted to communicate with these potential forces and utilize a massive translator equipped with most of the world's extinct and extant languages.

Jett remembered the conversation with Dr. Soliz, which was still fresh on his mind when he was asked to install a transmitter on top of one of their jeeps. It was windy that day, and Dr. Soliz kept adjusting the transmitter to receive and transmit signals just right.

It happened without warning. A group of orbs descended over the Pyramids, and the soldiers with them took position and recalibrated the weapon from the Sphinxes. Dr. Soliz had lectured the soldiers not to open fire on any force unless instructed by Jett or Corporal Balco to do so.

Never before had Jett seen the orbs act so unencumbered despite the arid environment. Jett put on some sunglasses, especially fitted to filter out harmful radiation or other harmful effects. These orbs were distinct from the others. When Jett used the magnification device on his sunglasses, he could see what looked like appendages—like they were testing out their environment. Dr. Soliz began to punch in codes and words into the transmitter. The transmitter beeped, but nothing happened initially, despite Dr. Soliz's knowledge that a reaction would occur within the first fifteen minutes.

It happened quickly. Jett was on top of the jeep when suddenly one of the orbs flew towards him. It took one of its appendage-like arms and scooped Jett up. The orb was cool to the touch despite its brightness and illusions of extreme heat.

"Jett, don't move," screamed Helen.

"I can't help it," he said.

Jett was squirming in the grip of the orb.

The orb appeared to be irritated as it began to pulse. Jett pulled his legs away from the orb, but it was too late; its heat singed them. They were cool to the touch on the outside, but towards the center, they were heated.

He ran his hand through his shorts. He found a scanner and a sampler. Scanning the orb, he returned the information to Dr. Soliz and the camp. The scanner did not provide him with much information, but it had not detected anything overtly dangerous yet. The team down by the Pyramids will make the decision. He placed the sampler in the orb and drew it from its brightness. After a couple of minutes, Jett looked at the results. It was made of plasma. Therefore, there may be a way to eliminate or reverse these phenomena, returning them to their original state in whatever universe they originated from.

As he drew closer to the orb, he could not help but think about the fate of his father and Peter. Was this it? What was it like to die? He heard Helen's scream and the explosions that rocked the outermost layers of the orb. Jett went unscathed despite the explosions practically exploding on top of him.

The mission crossed his mind as he nudged more information into this scanner. There was not much life left in him. He searched his pockets for anything that might aid him. He found something. It was a sample from the petroglyph site. He threw it into the orb.

The orb fell silent, and then it quaked, dropping Jett onto the ground with a thud. Jett looked up and realized that the fall could have killed him, but for some reason, it didn't. It was not his time, he thought. He heard Dr. Soliz calling his name.

"Jett, should we open fire?" Dr. Soliz asked.

He saw the soldiers staring at him. Helen was running in his direction and carrying medical supplies. He tried to shout, but he coughed up blood instead. He was wounded after all. He tried not to move. The orb rose back into the sky with the others, and Jett couldn't help but admire its beauty. Jett lacked the strength to give the order to open fire on the orbs.

"Jett, it's me, Helen," a voice said. A soldier accompanied Helen.

Jett could tell he was going in and out of consciousness. Helen looked beautiful as she always did. Her hair was swept up with the yellow dust and winds. She looked tranquil despite the urgent situation.

"Jett, can you hear me? "Where are you hurt?" Helen asked.

"I can hear you. " I feel like I hurt my side," Jett said.

"I have some scissors, Helen. We need to open up his shirt to check for internal bleeding, and I will also start an IV," said the soldier.

"Do we have supplies to treat him?" Helen asked the soldier.

"Yes, we do," said the soldier confidently.

Jett's surroundings were faint, but he could pick out the most minor details around him. Helen and the soldier set him up, and he looked straight ahead, but he should not have. In the distance, a group of men in black masks, hoodies, and pants was running towards them. Jett did not have the strength to fight but leaned over to Helen. He saw Corporal Balco and Lieutenant Radisson on top of the jeep with guns and weapons.

"Tell Dr. Soliz to open fire on those men," said Jett.

XIII

Corporal Balco and Lieutenant Radisson let the guns rip into the sand and eventually hit the men. Several soldiers from the team ran up to them and arrested them. Jett grabbed Helen's and the other soldier's shoulders and made his way to the camp around the jeeps.

"Find out who they are with," said Jett to Corporal Balco and Lieutenant Radisson.

It took some convincing, but the soldiers eventually got some of the men in black clothing to reveal information about who had sent them and why. They were with the Sphinxes, and they were locals. They said it was more of an independent job because they had heard what was at stake.

When he was on a medical bed at the camp beside the jeep, he asked for Corporal Balco. Jett felt he needed to continue the mission despite his injury, the orbs, and the intrusions. He told Corporal Balco to ask Helen to follow Dr. Soliz's orders.

"We need to stick to the mission," said Corporal Balco.

"For all we know, everyone at Command may be dead. Communication was vital with them, and now we are on our own. We need to send out random messages to whoever we captured William Sono," said Jett.

"But that will reveal that we are in Egypt?" questioned Corporal Balco.

"We must do it," said Jett.

"Alright," said Lieutenant Radisson.

Dr. Soliz was conducting additional tests on the weapon that would release energy at the top of the Pyramids. Helen was with Maria's family, tending to Dr. Soliz's stations. Dr. Soliz harnessed the family's unused potential by teaching them some of the essential workings of his equipment. Calculations were performed using the equipment regarding the Anomaly or miasma. Jett had gone over to the equipment stations to help decipher the calculations Dr. Soliz and the family were doing.

The Anomaly had indeed spread across Egypt toward the Pyramids. The orbs were still above them, holding steady like sentinels from some science fiction book. Jett had developed the miasma theory for the Anomaly, but it had yet to be proven. Dr. Soliz was finally turning all the theoretical musings the team had gathered since contact with the various forces. Dr. Soliz wanted to send an energy pulse to the top of the main Pyramid. Even though this would destroy the top of the pyramid, Dr. Soliz was hoping for some reaction from the vessel in Galveston, TX.

Sono was locked up in the back of Corporal Balco's jeep. Jett decided to go over to him to interrogate him further about the drugs, the infiltrations into the world, and the US government. There was not much time to find out any more information from Sono.

"Sono, what are the Sphinxes doing with the drugs?" said Jett.

Sono snarled and laughed.

"The same thing you are doing right now, bringing the Anomaly closer to you when it should go away. You are only doing it to yourselves," Sono said.

"What do you mean?" inquired Jett.

"The Sphinxes were aware of your miasma theory, Jett. We discovered it before you did. It was in our organization's teachings about injustices and powers from beyond this world," said Sono.

"What will the Anomaly, the miasma, do?" said Jett.

"It will destroy you. Consume you," laughed Sono.

Jett grew frustrated and felt like punching him. Sono sat in the back of the jeep and continued to laugh. Jett had had enough, and he punched Sono's side and stomach. He knocked the wind out of him, and Sono stopped laughing. Sono looked at him with amusement still.

"That's some punch you've got there, Jet, but you're feeding more into the plot of these forces and the Sphinxes." Remember, you are the key: you and your girl. The government is the one that got you. Remember," said Sono.

The jeep lurched suddenly, and Sono did not grow quiet; instead, he laughed even louder. The ground quaked, and Jett heard the family's screams. Jett wanted more information from Sono and figured he would get it only if he pried more into Sono's mind.

"Why do you say I'm the key?" said Jett to Sono.

"You're what the forces want; you're unique to them. Every time you do something wrong that increases the power of the Anomaly, it grows. The Sphinxes never cared for what the troops wanted. The Sphinxes are just interested in the drugs," said Sono.

"Why me?" said Jett.

"You lost your family, your best friend, and they may even go after your girlfriend. I do not know what they want, but it seems to be the end of the world. However, as I mentioned, we, the Sphinxes, could not care less," said Sono.

"You sound overly assured of yourself," said Jett.

"Well, I know the Sphinxes and our allies will win. As we are speaking, the Sphinxes have released the drugs into the major water systems of major cities. Soon, the world will be under our control," said Sono.

Jett immediately got up and ran over to Dr. Soliz. He wanted more information about the drugs, but Jett could tell there was not much time, as the orbs in their eerie light looked agitated again. Helen was beside him, assisting some soldiers with data collection.

"Jett, glad to see you," Dr. Soliz said.

"How is our progress going?" said Jett.

"We are about to fire the weapon at the top of the Pyramid. It should have the desired effect," said Dr. Soliz

"Helen, I need to talk to you about the Sphinxes for one quick moment," Jett said.

"Alright, what is it?" Helen said.

"Sono—he said the Sphinxes have released the drug into the major water systems of cities worldwide," said Jett.

"Is there an antidote?" questioned Helen.

A look of frustration grew over Jett's face.

"We haven't had time, Helen, to develop an antidote. He also said they could be after you, so be cautious," Jett said.

"Understood," Helen said.

Everyone put their gear on and took positions in the jeeps and throughout the new camp as Dr. Soliz was almost ready to fire the weapon. At Dr. Soliz's station, Jett felt the device's vibrations. Dr. Soliz gave the cue to Lieutenant Radisson and Corporal Balco, and he fired the weapon. The weapon's light was almost more brilliant than the light from the orbs. Instead of the top of the pyramid exploding, it retained the energy it was exposed to.

The energy appeared to collect at the top and then rapidly pulse. For a moment, Jett thought the orbs appeared attracted to the pulsating light on top of the Pyramid. One of the orbs removed one of its appendages again and touched the top of the pyramid. A loud, ear-piercing crackle was heard as the orb made contact with the top.

A boom was also heard, and the orb shifted, lowering itself to the ground. Dr. Soliz ordered another shot at the top of the pyramid, and the orb came down further. It collapsed to just above the ground and hovered there.

"I think we should fire on the orb just above the ground," said Dr. Soliz.

"Don't you think that's a bit aggressive?" Jett said.

"We need to know what they are. They can be stopped, but we need to know," Dr. Soliz said.

The energy device was trained on the orb, and the energy hit it, causing a loud boom to be heard again. The orb crashed to the ground. Jett was stunned. It was not just an orb of plasma energy. It had a metal shell.

"Just as I thought," Dr. Soliz said.

Jett felt skeptical about what Dr. Soliz said. The orb appeared to be damaged. Was it partly alive like the one back in Galveston, Texas, Jett thought. He performed his calculations and walked over to Corporal Balco.

"Do you think this orb has similarities to the vessel in Galveston?" said Jett.

"I don't know. But, look!" Corporal Balco pointed.

Several soldiers also turned to look at the orb, which was shaking. Towards the bottom of the orb, it appeared like a door had opened. Behind the door-like opening, a figure appeared, although Jett could not tell who or what it was. The other two orbs had also descended from the sky. These orbs seemed to have escaped the energy pulse emanating from the top of the Pyramid. There was not much Jett could do but watch the orbs hover above the ground for a while.

Dr. Soliz was frantically trying to take pictures and fumbling with his devices. He looked nervous and shooed several soldiers and Helen away from his equipment. Helen ran over to Jett.

"Dr. Soliz says this is it? We either get our answer or we don't," said Helen.

"I'm betting we're going to get an answer, but it may not be one we like," said Jett.

Helen watched with Jett for over an hour. The orbs barely moved, and nothing appeared from the door. Jett decided to go to Corporal Balco for direction on what to do next about the situation.

"I think we should give the orbs a whomping from the energy pulse," Corporal Balco said.

"We don't want to harm them, so we need to hold off as much as we can," said Jett.

"I know, but we can't let anything more happen," said Corporal Balco.

"Just give it another hour," said Jett.

Twilight was near the Pyramids in another hour, and the orbs emitted vibrant colors and a light display in the near darkness. When Jett approached, Dr. Soliz was in the back of one of the jeeps. Jett saw he was taking a break and grew irritated.

"Why aren't you at your station, Dr. Soliz?" said Jett.

"I needed a break. I let Lieutenant Radisson take over," Dr. Soliz said.

"Do you think anything will happen in a couple of hours or later tonight?" said Jett.

"This is our prime opportunity. There have been increasing reports from around the world of peaceful interactions with the orbs. We still don't know the causes of the other forces, the Anomaly and El Diablo," said Dr. Soliz.

Jett and Dr. Soliz were in the midst of a conversation when an alarm sounded near Dr. Soliz's equipment at Lieutenant Radisson. Several soldiers ran past Jett, and light began to shine everywhere. He ran over to where Lieutenant Radisson was, but before he could get there, a bolt of light or energy emerged from the orb with the door and struck Lieutenant Radisson and the equipment, sending Jett and the soldiers to the ground.

When Jett finally got up, there was dust everywhere, and when he looked further, Lieutenant Radisson and the other soldiers had been turned to a pile of ash. The door had opened, but Jett did not consider this a warm welcome.

Helen was also sent crashing to the ground, and she got up and ran towards him.

"Jett, what do we do?" said Helen.

"We need to stay calm. Dr. Soliz said we are making progress," Jett said.

"Progress?! "This is not progress," Helen said.

"But, there is progress now," said Jett.

"Jett, we need you to go to Sono and figure out what we can do about the drug in the water systems. There have been riots in the streets of Cairo," Corporal Balco said.

The pile of ash blew in the wind. Jett looked away and put a cloth that he had found in his pocket on his face. Corporal Balco and some others were still monitoring the door that had opened on the damaged orb.

What came from the direction of the door was not a glob; it was more like a form of a tall man with long fingers and toes. When the figure moved, its globular appearance pulsated and stayed in one place despite the strong winds of the desert. It stood there for some time like an awakened hawk about to search for prey. Or, was it?

Nothing frightened Jett more than a mystery; what he saw was a mystery. This was a new life Dr. Soliz, Jett, and the others had encountered. This newfound scientific feeling Jett was getting was exhilarating, but it did not sit right with him. In the best possible world, Jett did not believe any creature meant harm on purpose, like Dr. Soliz or Sono may suggest.

There was something more to the new life form that they were encountering.

Helen raised her camera to her face and looked through it. She snapped a picture without a flash. Corporal Balco ordered the jeeps back past the camp. They had established what was left of the contingent of soldiers that had been with them.

"Jett, we need to approach this smartly," barked Corporal Balco.

"I know; there is much we could learn; I don't think that person or thing has all the answers, though," said Jett.

"We cannot mess this up. Get Helen to contact Command immediately," said Corporal Balco.

"Marvelous, just marvelous," said Dr. Soliz as he walked over to where Jett and Corporal Balco were.

"Congratulations on your discovery, Dr. Soliz," said Jett.

"That is, it is our discovery, nothing more. I couldn't have done it without you," said Dr. Soliz.

"Helen, contact command about our new friend from the orb, and the news that the Sphinxes have released drugs into the water systems of major cities," said Jett.

"I'm on it," said Helen.

Helen ran back to where the jeeps were. Dr. Soliz, Corporal Balco, and Jett stood at the edge of the camp. The three of them marveled at the being assessing its surroundings. The being bent its neck and then pointed its head—or what seemed like it-up, and when the being did that, a large eye opened up and looked over its globular mass.

"What do we do, communicate with Morse code with this thing? Look at that eye!" said Corporal Balco.

"It's uncanny, isn't it. We've been searching for so long, and life finally found us," said Dr. Soliz.

"Do you think it knows we are here?" said Jett.

"Definitely," said Dr. Soliz.

Concern washed over Jett. The others seemed mesmerized by what they were seeing and not taking into account all the lives lost, mayhem, and destruction caused by these visitors. His father and Peter passed through his mind.

"The greater question is who started everything," said Jett.

"Sounds like you are taking this more as a fight than a discovery," said Dr. Soliz.

"I want that to be true, Dr. Soliz, but we cannot have the best of both worlds. Whatever world this being is from," said Jett.

The light from orbs shone brightly, and as time wore on, it was clear no one was about to get any sleep. Helen had heard back from Command, and they were ordered to make contact with the being because they, too, had heard about the plot of the Sphinxes. Some of the major cities in America had already fallen under the mind-control substance of the Sphinxes. Jett felt the weight of the discovery but knew the Sphinxes were winning, and action must be taken or they would lose everything, including the encounter with the being. He walked over to the back of one of the jeeps, where Helen was, when something came out of the corner of his eye.

XIV

It was more like a shadow at first. Jett was looking at Helen, who was gorgeous as always. In that moment, everything seemed to slow down, and Jett felt the pressure of a pinch on his left shoulder. After he felt the pinch, everything snapped back into reality. It was a bullet that had grazed him.

"Get down, Jett," said Helen.

Corporal Balco crouched down on the ground and returned some fire. He managed to make it to Jett with only one soldier. The others were taken down in the attack.

"It's the Sphinxes. Sono isn't under guard. I'm going to send my last man to stand by him," said Corporal Balco to Jett.

"I understand," screamed Jett over the fire of bullets. "I think they are after Helen, though."

Corporal Balco, Helen, and Jett hid underneath the Jeep. Corporal Balco was nearer to the open than they were and looked to see how many attackers there were. Corporal Balco scanned the area and the horizon. The bullets were coming from the shantytown near the city's border.

"Damn, they must be under that mind-control. They look like armed civilians," said Corporal Balco.

"We don't have time for this, Corporal Balco," said Jett.

"I know. You said they were after Helen, so I'm trying to think," said Corporal Balco.

"Where's Dr. Soliz?" said Jett.

"I told him to take cover at his station. That's the last I knew of his status," said Corporal Balco.

"Jett, I think being is more important. We need to get to it somehow," said Helen.

"You are crazy, Helen. You don't know what that thing is. It could kill you," said Corporal Balco.

"It's what the Sphinxes are after and controlling. Why don't you give them to me and find out what you can with the being," said Helen.

"Too late," said a voice.

Someone grabbed Corporal Balco by the neck and hoisted him up, and Jett heard a punch. Blood trickled down onto the yellow sand, and Corporal Balco dropped with a thud. Jett tried to grab the stranger's boots, but they moved out of his reach.

Suddenly, more men surrounded the jeeps, pulling Helen and Jett out into the open. They grabbed Helen by the chin and put a knife to it. Jett was bound by some rope behind his back, and a cloth was put into his mouth.

Sono raised his hands and signaled the other attackers. They grabbed Helen and took her toward the shantytown, where Jett could see other vehicles. He looked into the eyes of the armed civilians. Some looked like they were clearly out of control. The mind-control drugs had been a success.

The attacks struck a pole to the ground and tied Jett and Corporal Balco to it. When they took Helen, she was quiet, but she was kicking the assailants as she was led off into the distance. It was scorching hot, and the sand irritated Jett's eyes. Jett saw he had dropped an object in the sand and kicked some of the sand away. It was a pocket knife he had brought with him. He maneuvered down the pole to the sand and grabbed and picked up the knife. He cut through the rope, tied him together, and set Corporal Balco free.

Dr. Soliz was heard in the distance screaming their names. Jett grabbed up their walkie-talkies and radioed into Dr. Soliz. Oddly enough, the orbs were still there, and so was the being. Dr. Soliz was shouting something incoherently. Jett turned the walkie-talkie to Dr. Soliz.

"Jett, are you okay?" said Dr. Soliz

"No, Corporal Balco and I had been tied to a pole for a while, but we are fine. How is our friend and the orbs?" said Jett.

"They have been communicating, Jett, but from what I can tell, it is not good," said Dr. Soliz.

"I understand. They were shot out. Go figure, and William Sono and the attacks took Helen," said Jett.

"They took her?! We need her Jet," said Dr. Soliz.

"I know," said Jett, "I have a hunch, though, that Sono and them will quickly resurface."

"Well, I'll give you some time to take it all about Helen," said Dr. Soliz.

"We don't have all day," chimed in Corporal Balco.

"Corporal Balco's right, Dr. Soliz, therapy can wait. We also have to figure out what to do about the drugs entering the water systems of the major cities," said Jett.

Jett and Corporal Balco approached Dr. Soliz's station and analyzed his findings. Jett pored over the findings until he got the courage to address Dr. Soliz about his discovery. Jett was stunned and did not know how to react to the situation.

"Dr. Soliz, so these beings are multi-dimensional?" said Jett.

"That's right, they are not of our dimension," said Dr. Soliz.

"Can we kill them?" said Corporal Balco.

"Kill. No. They aren't harming anyone yet. Science says animals will only strike when hungry, harmed, or in danger," said Dr. Soliz.

"And, that means?" said Corporal Balco with a raised eyebrow.

"That means I am sticking with science and following testable facts. I think these beings are in danger, have been harmed, or hungry—so to speak," said Dr. Soliz.

Jett furrowed his brow in anger. He did not have time for Dr. Soliz's theories and facts. Jett knew his theory still held sway since he was on this mission. However, the situation had already passed through some theories, and his theories were about the miasma.

Looking at the being from Dr. Soliz's station, Jett looked at its titan figure. It was from somewhere. For some reason, he felt anger go up and down his spine again. He looked around at Dr. Soliz and Corporal Balco, who were looking at instruments. They are the enemy, thought Jett.

He ran to the energy device, fired it at the pyramid, and aimed it at the lowest orb and the being. The device was powering up when Corporal Balco noticed him, and Corporal Balco shouted at him. Jett's hands held tightly over the controls.

"Jett, get down from there," said Corporal Balco.

"This needs to be done," said Jett.

"What are you talking about? We are close to understanding this discovery?" said Corporal Balco.

"There's nothing you can do if you go that route," said Jett.

And, with that, Jett fired the weapon at the lowest orb and the being. Jett blinked. He did not know what had happened, but he was on his back in the sand by the device. He could still hear the sounds of the orbs. He sat out and looked around him.

Corporal Balco and Dr. Soliz were lying on the ground. They were now getting up, like he was, and looking themselves over. Jett felt a familiar presence beside him. The sunshine was still blotting out his vision as he looked around and felt someone's hand on his shoulder. He turned abruptly around. It was Peter.

Peter smiled. Jett wanted to scream with joy and fear. He had been there when Peter had died.

"It's me, Jett. It's Peter," said Peter. His voice was the same, and he wore the same clothes as the day he died. On seeing Peter, Corporal Balco readied his weapon.

"Hold on, Corporal Balco," said Jett as he got up. "It's Peter." "It's not," said Corporal Balco.

"I don't believe it. It's you, Peter! What happened?" said Jett.

"Jett, I believe you are mistaken. Take a look around you," said Dr. Soliz.

Jett looked around him and noticed the door to the lowest orb was closed, and the being was missing. Wispy clouds flew in the sky, and the sand glowed with the intense shine of the orbs. Jett wiped his hands clean of the sand and grabbed Peter's hand. Peter caught and pulled him up, but the dream ended when Jett touched Peter's eyes.

"You're not, Peter," said Jett. Jett looked deeply into Peter's eyes; instead of Peter looking back, it was someone or something else.

"It's me, Jett. Don't you remember me?" said Peter sorrowfully.

"No, it's not. Peter is dead," shouted Jett.

Peter suddenly breathed on Jett, and his breath was cold, not warm, confirming his suspicions. Jett grabbed Peter and then pushed him away. He did not want anything to do with this.

"Who are you? What are you?" said Jett.

"I'm your friend, Jett," said Peter.

"You're not," cried Jett. Tears fell on his face. "You were taken, Peter."

"Taken? I've always been here, Jett. You're forgetting. This whole thing has been one bad memory," said Peter.

Memory. That's it, though, Jett. What was he doing before he ended up on the sand? Jett stood there, puzzled for a while, and searched his mind. He remembered the orbs, but there was something else missing. He got angry, and it was about Peter. But there was something else. Jett poked at Peter. Peter's body was cold, too.

"Jett, snap out of it. This isn't Peter," said Corporal Balco.

Jett looked at Corporal Balco, who was holding a weapon. Jett looked up and remembered he was on the device, shooting at the being and the lowest orb. Jett looked at Peter again.

"It's you. The alien," said Jett.

Peter's face and body shifted right in front of Jett. Peter's smile turned into a sneer, and Jett could not stand where the alien stood. It smelled. Corporal Balco had his weapons trained on the alien. Dr. Soliz was circling them with their devices.

"What do you want?" said Jett to the alien.

"We want what you want, Jett, a life, a home," said the alien.

"Do you have a name?" said Jett.

"We don't have names like your kind," said the alien. "If it were a name, it would be more like saying you're pronoun 'I' or 'me.' We are all I or me."

"We haven't harmed you in any way," said Jett furiously, "But you have taken someone from every one of us here right now. You have taken something from the world—our world."

"Your world," said the alien, "My kind of humans are presumptuous, but not that much. We don't think this is your world anymore. But it is ours," said the alien.

"That is not what I meant. And, you need a name, so I'll call you Stan," said Jett.

"Okay, but I still will have to kill the three of you," said Stan.

"Wait, you do not understand. We have done *nothing* to harm you," said Jett adamantly.

Stan stood there unblinking with the eye at the center of his forehead. The door to the lowest orb opened up, and more aliens came out, who looked exactly like Stan. Dr. Soliz ran over to get a better view.

"You know about the Sphinxes, right, Stan? They are the ones trying to harm you. They are trying to trick you into taking over our world," said Jett.

"And, how would they manage that?" said Stan bluntly.

"They have connections high in Earth's world governments. Even the US President has been linked to their doings," said Jett.

Stan fell silent, and a hum began to enter Jett's ear. He thought his ears were ringing, but it was more like a controlled noise with a beat. He looked at Stan, whose color looked peaceful. For an alien who had few facial features, Jett somehow knew Stan's mood.

"You need to come with me, Jett," said Stan.

Jett looked around. Corporal Balco still had his weapon trained on Stan, and Dr. Soliz was still keeping his distance. Jett went over to Stan's side and motioned for Corporal Balco to lower his gun and for Dr. Soliz to take a step back away from Stan. Stan needed to know he was safe.

"Corporal Balco, I'm going with Stan," said Jett.

"Who's Stan?" questioned.

"He's the alien right before you," said Jett.

"You need to be safe, Jett, and that isn't," said Dr. Soliz.

"Where is he taking you?" said Corporal Balco.

"To their orb, to their ship, I think," said Jett.

Stan motioned with his long, multicolored hands for Jett to move toward the ship. Jet began walking with Stan. Stan wasn't walking, though. It was more like he was floating. Stan returned some power to Dr. Soliz's equipment as he passed by his station.

"Stan, you must help me get back my friend from the Sphinxes, the criminal organization doing this to everyone, you and me," said Jett.

"Who is your friend?" said Stan.

"Her name is Helen. She was taken by the Sphinxes when you appeared," said Jett.

Stan remained silent. His iridescent appearance shimmered in neither delight nor fury, just a slow, steady pulse which countered the pulse of the orb they were approaching. Jett stood right up to the orb. The orb's glow was not intense, even though Jett was beside it. He touched the wispy plasma, and it was neither hot nor cold. Stan was already walking up to the door, and he was standing inside the entryway. Jett ran up to the entryway and looked behind him. The Saharan sand was littered with charred debris remains, and some stations were still on fire. He knew he must go inside now.

When he was inside the orb, it was neither spacious nor small. It seemed the right size all the time—at least to him. Jett looked at Stan, and the alien had retained his stature. Stan looked like he was working with some instruments on the orb. Further staring into the orb, it looked like nothing was there, like the orb in Galveston.

Jett stretched out his hands, and his hand went through some plasma passing him. He continued to follow Stan. He also noticed there was no center or walls of the orb. Looking behind him, Jett noticed there was no evidence of the door. So much for a quick way out, Jett thought.

"Over here, Jett," motioned Stan.

Perspiration began to collect on Jett's forehead. There were environmental systems here, thought Jett. Stan brought him to what Jett could tell was several feet forward. Jett started to lose his bearings without knowing where the center was, and there were no walls. Stan touched Jett's forehead, and calm went throughout his body. They both stood for a while.

"What would you like to know, Jett?" said Stan.

"Well, why are you here? Why did you attack us? Why is this all happening?" said Jett.

"Very well," said Stan in a comforting voice.

Stan waved his hand in front of him, and a mirror or a water-like slab appeared. Jett peered into it, and he could see Earth from space. He grew nervous since he had not noticed if the orb had taken flight.

"My kind are from an alternate dimension. We are multi-dimensional, to be exact. Our kind were much like humans hampered by our circumstances, but we surpassed them with time and effort," said Stan.

"Well, why are you here on Earth?" said Jett.

Stan seemed flustered by this question, and his colors changed. The view from the water-like slab took a view of Earth. This view of Earth looked scarred, barren, and on fire.

"Do you recognize what you are looking at?" said Stan.

"It's Earth, but it looks like it has gone through some kind of devastation," said Jett.

"Your devastation," Stan said pointedly.

Jett recoiled. Stan the alien, or whatever he was, was showing something that had not happened yet. He grew impatient and touched the slab.

He immediately felt a jolt of energy, and the slab became images of somewhere else—a similar place to the orb, without distance. The image seemed to communicate to Jett that this was Stan's home.

XV

Jett stared into the distance, or the lack of it now. There was no sound, only light and color. He looked down and found he was floating more than anything. He turned to his right, and Stan was still there, thankfully. Looking further around him, Jett saw there was another alien with him. It was like Stan, although it was more preoccupied with another mirror-like slab next to him.

"This is your home, Stan?" said Jett.

"It is, Jett," said Stan.

Massive plumes of what looked like plasma or some strange multi-dimensional substance erupted in the midst of where Jett and Stan were standing. Jett caught one of the plumes in his hands, and it turned into a dog. Jett laughed at this magical element in this new place. Stan signaled for Jett to move forward, but suddenly there was a hum and then a boom. A whoosh of plasma went by Jett. Some more plasma went by Jett, and the more Jett saw, the more he concluded it all was being pulled in by some force. Stan's colors had grown somber with concern, and the other alien as well. There was another boom then a lurch. A bright light was seen in front of Jett, and he held his hands up to cover his eyes and moved closer to Stan. Jett saw a hole in the multi-dimensional space through his fingers.

He looked further into the world as it grew larger. He could see the whole of Earth, and it zoomed in on the continent of North America. Then he was in the White House. The Sphinxes were in the White House, holding some people hostage.

"What is going on, Stan?" said Jett.

"It seems like your assertion that the Sphinxes are a threat is held as valid," said Stan.

"Why is there a hole here?" said Jett.

"Our world is being damaged through activities in your world," said Stan.

"Like this one?" said Jett.

"Not all," said Stan.

A stench filled the multi-dimensional area, and Jett covered his face. Another hole opened up to the far east of them. If such a thing existed in this place, thought Jett. In this hole, though, a manufacturing plant was seen with all its smoke and pollution. Another boom and lurch happened, and a hole opened on top of the other one. But, in this hole was a mound of trash next to the ocean and dead or struggling marine life.

"What does this mean, Stan?" said Jett

"Do you not know? Your planet is dying from your kind actions. And, my kind are dying too because of it. These holes are ruptures in our multi-dimensional space, but we have managed to utilize them to see what is going on, but they keep appearing," said Stan.

"So, we are harming you?" said Jett

"Yes," said Stan.

"But why attack us?" said Jett.

"There was no way for us to respond without damage to your world. Plus, there are fractions of us that do what to annihilate your kind because of your actions," said Stan.

"While that may be true, Stan, I still have a lot of questions? Like the Anomaly and El Diablo. I had my theory about the Anomaly. I linked it to miasma, which humans use to explain away science. The Anomaly functioned like ancient human mythology," said Jett.

"The Anomaly is our world merging into yours," said Stan.

Something about Stan's mode of speech unsettled Jett. It was like hearing an echo, and Jett also knew Stan was inside his mind, somehow. He wanted to say a lot to Stan, but he knew he was understanding despite the overwhelming images Jett was seeing now.

The place where Stan, Jett, and the other aliens lurked again. The plasma-like substances seemed to zoom out suddenly, and Jett was near the door again, which got him into the orb. The other alien was with them, although this time, Stan's colleague was crouching down and holding himself. It seemed to be in pain. Stan looked at him, and his colors changed in a flurry of different light strobes and plasma bursts.

Jett still wanted his answer about the Anomaly. "So, the Anomaly is your world merging into ours. But what brought it? The Anomaly seemed only enticed by whatever was happening in the world. It was a pattern," said Jett.

"You're observant, astute, and correct," said Stan.

"What about the Anomaly and everything else?" said Jett.

"That is our coming," said Stan.

"What do you mean?" said Jett.

"It's our reality losing. We can do nothing to prevent it. It just is," said Stan.

"But, the Anomaly, it's a way response of your kind to what?" said Jett.

"It's a response to the hurt and pain caused to the Earth. It demands justice," said Stan.

Jett looked over at the other alien. At that moment, some other aliens were joining near the doorway Stan and Jett were standing next to. Jett noticed some aliens were holding themselves, and some were hobbling to the door.

"We are losing, Jett," said Stan.

"How do you know?" inquired Jett.

"Some of my kind are falling ill with too much exposure to your reality. We weren't meant to have lasted this long, either of our kind. But we have," said Stan.

"What about Earth?" said Jett. "It will last, won't it? Something will be left?"

"Come this way, Jett," calmly said Stan.

Stan took him to one of the mirror slabs, and Jett peered in, but all he could see was soil and dirt. Stan motioned to him, but first, Stan placed his hand over the soil. Green sprouts immediately shot up, and flowers sprang up from the soil.

"You have listened to the Earth, Jett, and it has given you some power. Use it wisely," said Stan.

The slab switched to another view of the soil, and Jett ran his hands through it. It was real. He clumped up the soil and let it sift through his fingers. He watched different flowers and grasses spring up before him. Jett's eyes began to water. The Earth was saying something to him. It had been saying something to him his whole life. It was only now that he was listening.

The term space slipped his grasp with the next thing he saw, which was nothing. Jett looked around the black, eerie darkness. This darkness had replaced the plasma-like existence of the orb and the realm of Stan's kind.

"Anyone here?" Jett called out into the blackness around him.

"You are hiding from me. Aren't you, Stan?" But I can do that for more extended periods. I am smaller," said Jett.

There was no sound. Darkness and black surrounded Jett. He shoved his hands constantly in front of him to see if he would encounter anything. He did that for a time, and there was nothing. Jett was getting use to saying that word to himself—nothing, but he did not like it.

He had almost given up and began crouching to sit when he heard a purr. It was a loud purr. Not a purr like a house cat. It was something bigger. Earth was somewhere else, but there was something familiar about the sound. He had heard it at the zoo with the big cats there. He grew nervous thinking more and more about the purring sound. It would come close, then become distant. Jett pivoted where he stood and took a look around the blackness. There it was. For a moment, he thought he saw a shimmering black figure coming at him.

"Stan! Where are you?" cried out Jett.

Stan was not there to console him. Jett peered deeper into the darkness. He felt like something was there, watching him. The hairs on the back of his neck and his arms stood straight, and goosebumps followed. This was it, though, Jett. He was going to die here.

"What do you want? I know about the Sphinxes. I know about Stan and almost everything," said Jett.

"There's nothing that I want, Jett. I want only harmony and peace," said a voice.

Jett looked around in a frenzy. There was still nothing. He did not recognize the voice either. Finally, before him, he saw two yellow eyes. They looked like cat eyes.

He took some steps back, and perspiration covered his forehead. The head emerged from the darkness. It was a jaguar.

"You're back, the hallucinations. So, it is true, they have something to do with the aliens," said Jett.

"I am not a hallucination, Jett. You wouldn't be there if I were. This is simply a form of communication," said the Jaguar.

The jaguar's sleek body stealthily went around Jett. Jett froze and tried not to touch the jaguar. That was the thing about this hallucination or vision. It was tactile. The fur on the jaguar was as real to Jett as the darkness surrounding him. Jett cringed with fear as he could feel the warm breath of the jaguar on his face.

"So, what will you do, Jett?" said the Jaguar.

"First, I need to know who you are before I decide what to do," said Jett.

"This is Earth, the ecosystem, Gaia, communicating with you," said the Jaguar astutely.

"Okay, so what gives? Take me back, please," said Jett to the Jaguar.

"We—Earth—are intertwined with the aliens. You are hurting them and Earth along with it," said the jaguar.

"What is there to be done about it? It may be the end," said Jett.

"Do you remember when you and the aliens first met? You were with Helen, and the orbs appeared. Some men shot at you," said the Jaguar.

Jett thought a moment. He had almost forgotten how this all started, but never how deeply he wanted it to end. Jett couldn't lock eyes with the jaguar, but his neck hairs bristled with anger instead of fear now at the knowledge that the Sphinxes had taken Helen.

"Yes, I remember. That is one of the reasons why I am here now. The girl—Helen—was with me. She was taken shortly before I met you," said Jett.

"I see," said the Jaguar.

The Jaguar was proving not to be much help, Jett thought. The jaguar's presence only made him angrier that Helen was taken from him and his family. Helen would not want him to hold anger while he was on this mission. But, how could he? He was only human, and these were superhuman tasks. The Jaguar growled as it continued to look at Jett.

"I want to go somewhere. Is there a way?" said Jett.

"There is," said the Jaguar.

"I want to go to the place of one of the most powerful people on Earth. I want to go to Washington, D.C. to meet the president of the United States of America," said Jett.

"Why? They are the ones hurting us," said the Jaguar.

"No, they are being tricked—at least from what I know," said Jett.

"How so?" said the Jaguar.

"The Sphinxes, who I was told were the plot's culprit, have a mind-control substance and have put it into the water supplies of Earth's major cities. They may also have the United States President and other powerful governmental leaders under the influence of this drug," said Jett.

Calm came over Jaguar. It stood there momentarily and continued to eye Jett with less intensity, as if he was about to let him go and move on to more destruction or something. The Jaguar let out a roar, and two orbs buzzed into existence off to the side of the Jaguar. The orbs did their regular pulsation and color change.

"We will check this out by going to Washington, D.C. If this is true, we will find the Sphinxes, kill them, and end this problem with Earth," said the Jaguar.

"End the problem? There is no problem. You—the aliens—made yourself known to us first," said Jett.

"You have proved to be a problem," exclaimed the Jaguar in a roar. While the Jaguar roared, plasma around Jett shifted, and he felt suspended in the air. This suspension lasted for a while until he was there, touching a plane of existence.

"Turn around now," ordered the Jaguar.

"But, I don't take orders from anyone. I am on my mission," said Jett.

Suddenly, Jett felt pressure, and some force abruptly turned him. He was no longer facing the door he had entered initially on the orb, which opened to bright sunlight. He saw shades of green and other colors.

There was the Rose Garden of the White House. Jett did not know what to say; his order was fulfilled. Although he was standing in the Rose Garden, people set up chairs. He figured it was for a press conference.

"They cannot see you," said a voice.

"Who is this?" said Jett.

"It's me, the one you called Jaguar," said the voice.

"Okay, Jaguar, I want to go directly to the United States President. You will in time. He will be here any minute," said Jaguar.

More people came and set up chairs, brought in flags, and brought in a podium. They began filling in one after the other. Jett was impressed by their orderliness. Despite their formal attire, they looked worried. Some music started playing, and then Jett's person of interest.

The United States President looked tired in a traditional suit and tie, and his wrinkles amplified the worry that was strewn across his face. He stood there, clasping the podium and looking over the incoming guests and reporters. Jett completely forgot the protocol he had seen of the US President coming in after everyone was seated and everyone standing for him. This was no ordering press conference; Jett surmised there were television screens of maps of cities in the US and worldwide. A breeze swept through the garden, and rose petals flew across the president's chest.

"Good afternoon, everyone," said the President calmly. "Thank you for coming, and please excuse the informality. Some of our personnel have been taken from us recently."

His back stiffened, and he brought out a light pointer to do a presentation his way. This was President Schmidt after all. He got messy with his hands-on approach to his job, or nothing at all.

"As you can see here, the Anomaly and the activity in the sky, now called El Diablo, have further expanded," said the President. "There has been extensive civilian loss of life."

The crowd gasped and began scribbling in their notepads or typing on laptops. There was not much time for Jett to enjoy his invisibility. For one, he had a duty to do so, and for another, security personnel were already sweeping the area with scientific devices. He closed his eyes and felt Jaguar inside of him. Jett wanted to know how he could stop the Sphinxes and aliens. This was Earth speaking to him through the Jaguar. He knew now why he was picked for this monstrous mission.

XVI

The press conference lasted an hour, and Jett stood there the entire time. The security personnel had done their sweeps without detecting anything. Continuing with the press conference, President Schimdt began to answer questions from those present.

"President Schimdt, this is Hailey Kim with the New York Times. How do you account for the disappearance of the secretive mission to uncover and deal with forces behind all this?" said Ms. Kim.

"I am aware of the mission you speak of, and I will begin a full investigation of what happened to Operation Fire Marsh," said President Schimdt.

"Mr. President, when will more rations and other supplies be handed out to the American populations affected?" said another reporter.

President Schimdt's brow furrowed, and he pursed his lips. He seemed to be thinking. Jett removed his invisibility cloak so that there would not be so much of a surprise when a group of people stood. Jett made one final attempt to convince Jaguar to go back to Egypt.

"So, you sure about this Jaguar?" said Jett.

"I am certain we must make an impression on America and find out everything about President Schimdt," said Jaguar.

Jett moved to the right side of the reporter, standing, and suddenly became visible. Jett instantly wondered how long it would take everyone to catch on, given he had not changed clothes or showered. However, it seemed that Jaguar had gifted him new clothes and the feeling and smell of a fresh shower.

A slew of reporters asking for President Schimdt's attention soon followed some questions after Jett's appearance. Despite the tight security, he followed some White House staff details into the interior of the White House building. Jett looked around. President Schimdt had stopped to talk to some reporters about the specifics of Jett's mission's disappearance. He felt the presence of Jaguar looking through his eyes. The feeling was intense, like he knew who was predator and prey all at once, with some link to Earth around him.

There was an opening now to get the President. Jett knew he needed to strike, but how? He looked around as the reporters began to file out, and the President was just left with his staff. He conversed with the White House Press Secretary when Jett moved to place himself beside them.

"Jaguar, what should I do?" said Jett.

"You need to isolate him, and then we take him," said Jaguar.

"Take him? But, how?" said Jett.

"I'll handle the exit; You just handle the part of getting his attention and isolating him from the rest of the staff," said Jaguar.

"Alright," said Jett with less enthusiasm than he expected.

"Mr. President, you are needed in the Oval Office," said Jett.

President Schimdt politely raised his hand to the White House Press Secretary. He adjusted his suit and approached Jett, who was standing nearby. President Schimdt did not look bothered by anything but clapped his hands behind him and leaned into where Jett was.

"What is it? Make it quit," said President Schimdt.

"Follow me," said Jett.

They had rounded a corner, and that is when Jett sensed the presence of a Jaguar again. Everything around Jett was suddenly amplified, and he looked at President Schimdt. Jett was looking through the eyes of what Jett surmised was a Jaguar.

"Jaguar, what do I do?" said Jett.

"Touch him. Touch his hand or shoulder, and we will exit," said Jaguar.

"Okay," said Jett.

Jett extended his hand and touched President Schimdt's shoulder, and in a moment, they were back in the orb of plasma, but this time with the U.S. President. Jett saw Jaguar before him, looking at President Schimdt, who was looking around him in confusion. He spotted Jett between him and all the plasma.

"Where am I?" said President Schimdt.

"You're here to answer some questions, Mr. President," said Jaguar.

"And, you are a talking jaguar?" said the president questionably.

"That's right," said Jaguar.

"And, I'm Jett," said Jett as he moved closer to the president.

"You look familiar, Jett. I remember you on a mission roster. Were you assigned to Operation Fire Marsh?" said the President.

"Yes, I was," said Jett.

"Was? What happened to you? We were betting a lot on its success," said President Schimdt in a concerned voice.

"I've encountered some obstacles. We have contacted the aliens and learned the orbs are their ships and other information about the Anomaly and El Diablo. However, we have also learned there are politics and a criminal organization involved," said Jett.

"Well, whose side are you on in this conflict?" said President Schimdt.

Jett felt concern wash over him. He knew the operation he was on was primarily scientific, and he knew there was no debriefing on this being a conflict with known forces. Jett knew his subsequent statements and questions would change the president's attitude.

"We also know that high-ranking officials in the United States government, including you, have been implicated in the actions of the criminal organization, the Sphinxes," said Jett.

"I have done nothing wrong," said President Schimdt.

"So, I have been forced to take you hostage. The motivation is gone to obey you, Mr. President. I was almost killed by these aliens whose shop and realm you are now standing in, but I also lost many members of my team and Helen, a love interest of mine," said Jett.

"I empathize with your pain, Jett, but do not do anything brash. Hold your alliances and withdraw your efforts on holding me hostage, and this will all be forgotten. They will come for me, Jett, with all their might," said President Schimdt.

"I understand, President Schimdt, but there are millions, if not billions, of innocent lives at stake for your decisions," said Jett.

Despite what President Schimdt was saying, Jaguar was looking at him with the eyes of a predator. Jett still felt the presence of Jaguar in his thoughts. The Earth was helping Jett, but where was Stan? Jett looked into the orb. He could not see Stan. There were only vague forms of something or someone being there in the nebulous distance.

"Jaguar, we need to get more out of President Schimdt. We need evidence, or he will not go through with anything we have to say. We will have to deal with him by force, which is the worst option," said Jett.

"I know what to do and say, Jett. I'll remind him of Helen," said Jaguar.

Jaguar's voice was hopeful, but it was slipping. Jett could tell Jaguar was showing everything in his speech. President Schmidt's hands were still clasped behind his back. They had some handcuffs or manacles on them.

"Jaguar, what about Stan, the alien? I haven't seen him since we returned," said Jett curiously.

"Stan, is watching over for movement with the Sphinxes? We have to deal with President Schimdt alone," said Jaguar.

"I understand, Jaguar. Ask the President about Captain Meno and Galveston to see if he is on our side. That will reveal secrets. And the death of Peter. Was it ordered?" said Jett in his thoughts to Jaguar.

"Mr. President, do you remember two individuals named Captain Meno and Peter Vern?" said Jaguar.

"Again, I have no idea who you are talking about, but I do know about a Project Fire Marsh, but knowledge of that is protected by the highest levels of national security," said President Schimdt nervously.

Jaguar waved his paw, and the mirror-slab came over to where President Schimdt was. The new object caught President Schimdt's attention, and he leaned into it. He began to see the attack on the Command in Galveston and the fight with Peter. Worried lines crinkled on the sides of the eyes of President Schimdt, and he frowned.

"Do you or do you not remember this?" said Jett in a commanding voice.

"I will not respond to thugs or terrorists," said President Schimdt.

"Did you give the order to kill one of your members of the Operation Fire Marsh, Peter Vern?" said Jett.

President Schmidt's eyes frantically went side to side. The President was breaking, and Jett could see it now. However, Jett thought this was too easy.

"Peter Vern was in our way. And, for everything that has happened, the world is in our way," said President Schimdt.

"So, you also know about the mind-controlling drugs and how they kidnapped Helen, another member of Operation Fire Marsh," said Jett.

"It's all orchestrated. The world population is coming under our control and these things, these aliens, and eventually Earth," President Schimdt said firmly.

Coming near Jett, Jaguar began to shiver. Jett felt an intense fear coming from Jaguar. It was a fear of losing a battle, if not a war. This frightened Jett because he was alone in the orb without the guidance of Stan. Jett motioned for the mirror-slab to come to him.

"Where is Stan?" he said into the mirror-slab.

Immediately, an image of a dark grey temple surrounded by jungle appeared. Jett recognized the size and shape of this temple, Angkor Wat in Cambodia. Not many people were in the temple area, and Jett looked intensely to find some. He eventually looked by a group of trees, and he found some men hooded in black and Helen handcuffed to a nearby tree.

"Jaguar, we need Stan to get us to this location," said Jett.

"I understand, but the President has not given us the information we want yet," said Jaguar.

Jett looked closer into the mirror-slab and past the trees. He found William Sono standing over Helen, shouting at her. Helen looked badly beaten up from her experience. Sono was being tricky by going halfway around the world. Looking into the sky, Jett saw El Diablo approaching.

As Jett was standing above the mirror-slab, Stan materialized before him. His colorful demeanor was dull and erratic. Stan had learned what they needed to do next. There was not much time for musing over a decision. They had kidnapped the President, and decisions were required immediately.

"So, what do you want us to do, Stan? The mirror-slab found, Helen. She is in Cambodia," said Jett.

Stan went over to the mirror-slab, waved his hand over it, and closed it. He then materialized before President Schimdt. If it were not for the President's culpability in the matter at hand, Jett would say Stan was sizing him up for some game. But Satan was trying to intimidate him.

"Are you certain this is the one?" said Stan desperately to Jett and Jaguar. "As I am speaking, different factions have instituted war on the people of Earth, including the Sphinxes and your nation, Mr. President," said Stan harshly.

"Yes, he is the one," said Jett quickly.

"Then, open the door to the Pyramids in Egypt," said Stan.

A door appeared behind the President and kept floating forward towards him. Jett could tell it was ablaze with energy. The door grew large enough that the President had no choice but to enter it. Jett followed Jaguar.

Here they were again in the searing heat of Egypt's Sahara Desert. Jett looked around him and spotted the burned wreckage of his former mission. He took some steps toward it, hopefully to find Corporal Balco or Dr. Soliz. He looked inside one jeep and found Corporal Balco's old badge and Dr. Soliz's. This was a sign they had encountered someone or something.

"Where am I?" said the President.

As soon as the President saw the pyramids and the Egyptian sand, he scowled and began pacing back and forth. Jett looked up and saw that the two other orbs had ascended into the sky somewhere beyond the clouds. Stan was still standing beside President Schimdt, almost hovering over him. President Schimdt did not pay heed to Stan.

"You disobeyed all your orders, Jett, and got everyone killed," said President Schimdt.

"But I found you are one of the culprits, Mr. President," said Jett.

"There is no time for this talk. The factions of my kind are moving fast. The Anomaly and El Diablo, as you call them, will be throughout the world shortly, primarily in the remaining cities," said Stan.

Feeling Jaguar's presence inside his mind. Jett motioned for them to take seats around Dr. Soliz's station. That is when Jett heard them. It was the sound of the shifting sand that caught Jett's attention. He went about ten feet from the station. He prodded the sand with a discarded gun with no ammunition.

"Ow," said a voice.

Out of seemingly nowhere, Corporal Balco and Jett arose from the sand. They were well-cloaked, though Jett found them now. They both looked exhausted, but Jett was glad that he found them. Dr. Soliz's surprise was overtaken by a look of disgust on his face when he saw Stan standing there, but he was brought to attention when he saw President Schimdt.

"You're President Schimdt," said Dr. Soliz as he walked over to him

Dr. Soliz was not exactly happy with him since he confirmed his intelligence about his involvement with the Sphinxes. Corporal Balco drew his weapons and maneuvered over to the President. Jett held up his hands to Corporal Balco in a gesture that he was not harming the President, yet.

"There's more to this story, Corporal Balco," said Jett.

"How did the President get here? Jett, and it better not be by your doing. Or, the alien creep," said Corporal Balco.

"Corporal Balco, we also found Helen. She is in Cambodia with William Sono. We found the Sphinxes as well. They are there too," said Jett.

"So, he is here by his own will," said Corporal Balco.

"No, he is not," interrupted Stan.

"Shut up, creep," said Corporal Balco.

"Corporal Balco, please calm down. Stan can help. There is another thing you need to know while I was on their orb-ship," said Jett.

"And what exactly do I need to know, Jett?" said Corporal Balco.

"Some presence contacted me. This may sound ridiculous, but it's Earth communicating with me. It's like all those hallucinations we discussed on the ship back in

Galveston. It's here to help, and you need to know we are the ones hurting Earth and Stan—the aliens are somehow linked to the Earth, which brought them here," said Jett.

President Schimdt laughed out loud.

"Soldier, what is your rank?" said President Schimdt.

"I'm Corporal Balco, Mr. President," said Corporal Balco.

"This is well-above your authority and pay grade," said President Schimdt.

"He's well-suited for these duties, Mr. President," chirped Dr. Soliz to the President.

"You need to remember your allegiances, corporal. Now, get me out of these handcuffs," said President Schimdt.

Some booms were heard in the distance, and the orb they had exited from began to rise further from the desert sand. Jett looked up; four or five bigger orbs had appeared in the distance just past the Pyramids. Stan started moving to the orb that was rising. The earthquake rattled stones from the Pyramids.

"We must move now, Jett. The other factions of my kind are here. And, they will attack and kill," said Stan.

XVII

More stones went careening from the Pyramids. Stan held up his arms and deflected some of the rocks. Jett, sensing the President would not take his endangerment lightly, stood in front of Stan. He began asking him to protect President Schimdt with the power of the Jaguar, or nobody would survive.

The orbs beside them shot plasma at each other, and they moved into a position that looked like they were ready to take flight. Dr. Soliz gathered some final materials he had collected, but Stan signaled he would not need them. Dr. Soliz's eyes grew wide with amazement.

"I'm not going with them, Jett," said Corporal Balco.

"Corporal Balco, you must listen," said Jett. "The President was the one who ordered the attack on me and Helen when all of this first started, and he ordered Peter to die. He's been planning and directing this entire thing," said Jett.

"No, I don't believe you," said Corporal Balco. With that, Corporal Balco stood beside the president with a gun in hand. Stan was busy fending off the stones falling from the Pyramids. The booms and explosions had grown closer. Dr. Soliz took to Jett's side.

"Corporal Balco, don't do this; they will take the President anyway," said Dr. Soliz.

The orb in the middle had lowered again, and the doorway was preparing to open. Jett knew there was nothing more to do but to do something to Corporal Balco. He figured Jaguar would have something in mind for Corporal Balco's treachery.

"Jaguar, what do you suggest I do?" said Jett.

"I suggest taking some cover and going into the descending orb away from the oncoming factions," said Jaguar.

"Besides that!" said Jett hurriedly.

"I will simply get inside him like I am with you just now. I will take my Jaguar form, but remember only you, Stand, and he will be able to see me," said Jaguar.

"Alright," said Jett.

Corporal Balco armed himself and fired his gun at Stan. Jaguar appeared before Corporal Balco, and Corporal Balco shot some ammo into the air in surprise. Jaguar growled at Corporal Balco.

"There is no time for this Jaguar," said Stan upon seeing his move on Corporal Balco.

"Corporal Balco, you think this is implausible, but consider what you see. I don't want to take you out, but I will if the factions come too close. I need the president," said Jaguar.

At this point, Jett did not know if he was doing the right thing. Jaguar spoke with certainty, but Jett did not want to kill or harm Corporal Balco. Maybe President Schimdt was right that he was being tricked. He looked behind him as Dr. Soliz entered the orb.

"Jaguar, there is not much time! Do something!" said Jett over the roar of the oncoming factions.

Jaguar jumped right at Corporal Balco and disappeared. Corporal Balco was gripping his ears and head and screaming in pain. Corporal Balco looked up at Jett with bloodshot eyes.

"Jett, you promised," said Corporal Balco.

Corporal Balco then slumped down into the sand. He was dead. Jaguar appeared beside Jett. Jett felt that rage in him again. He had lost his entire original team. Was President Schmidt right?

"I told you, Jett, all this was a lie," said the President.

"You're coming with us," said Jett angrily.

They all moved back into the orb, and the door closed. Jett's last images of Egypt showed the Pyramids collapsing and fire engulfing the area on the ground he was previously on.

Jett could tell that the orbs were high in the sky. While in mid-flight, they were busy dodging El Diablo and other strange forces. Jett looked at the President, who had been slightly harmed while leaving Egypt. Jett went over to where Stan was and requested that someone heal the president.

"I'll get to that right away," said Stan.

Jett ordered a mirror-slab to appear before him, and he went to look for Helen and William Sono. Finding where they were flying to took some time, but they were flying east. The mirror-slab zoomed in on the Angkor Wat area. Jett immediately recognized Helen. She had been cleaned up and was free, although she was with guards. There were some Cambodians in the distance, but they were attacking erratically. There were perhaps just now coming under the effects of the mind-control substance.

Jett sat amid plasma as it whirled around him. Hours or minutes had passed since he looked in the mirror-slab to find Helen. He was trying not to place more guilt on himself since he lost Corporal Balco. The times were tense. Jett realized he and the president could be killed at a whim by Stan's kind or by Stan himself. Or, even by Jaguar.

"What are you thinking about?" said Stan.

"Helen, and how I need to let go if I do not fulfill my mission," said Jett.

"You will; Just think past all these obstacles. You were picked for a reason for this mission. You and your friends have done a great deal of good," said Stan.

"I know I am probably going through a bargaining stage or something with grief or something deeply psychological, but I am more realistic at heart, Stan. And, my gut is telling me we may not make it," said Jett.

"The probability of disaster is likely, but think of what has been gained. Contact with a form of life never discovered before and contact with another right beneath your feet," said Stan.

Jett felt the orb encounter something. Stan confirmed they had landed in Cambodia. The president began to shout and scream to release him, but Jaguar stood watch over him. The door appeared, and they all walked out with President Schimdt behind them.

When the plasma dissipated as they walked through the door, Jett saw immediately what he was encountering: a trap. The Sphinxes had already drawn guns, and William Sono stood there threateningly. Several local Cambodians were beside him with plasma guns. The plasma guns; that is how Jett knew even more was wrong. The advanced weaponry only existed at the Command on Galveston. Frantically, Jett looked past the dust caused by the landing and found some hostages with blindfolds on and guards by them. When he took steps toward Sono, Stan and Jaguar took steps with him.

"You're after someone; I can tell," said Sono.

"Maybe I am only here to fulfill my mission. Just release Helen and things will be toned down a bit," said Jett.

"Ah, the love of your life. But you have a bit more to worry about," said Sono. "Bring him."

Several Cambodians and Sphinxes brought over a man with a blindfold, whose profile Jett recognized as Captain Meno. A Sphinx took off the blindfold and revealed it was Captain Meno. The Sphinxes kicked him in the back and the back of the knees, sending him flying to the ground.

"What have you done, Sono?" said Jett.

"Command, it's been taken over," muttered Captain Meno.

He was grabbed by the head again and pushed to the ground and held there for a while. Some blood sputtered out of Captain Meno's mouth. Sono took a step, but then Stan raised a hand and halted Sono.

"I could kill you now," said Stan.

"And, I could seal you off from your kind. I could make it so that your kind will never be on Earth again," said Sono.

"Impossible, Earth needs us, and we need Earth. We will defend it with all the power of our kind," said Stan.

"Tsk, tsk, that is no way to talk to a future ruler of yours, whatever your name is," said Sono.

"The name is Stan. That is my given name now," said Stan as he looked at Jett.

Some locals were screaming in the distance; birds flew fast from the forest. Jett looked at Stan for an answer, but did not receive one, so he went to Dr. Soliz. Dr. Soliz had the last of his equipment out, and he was calculating what he could.

"What have you found, Dr. Soliz?" said Jett with concern.

"The miasma or the Anomaly, as we call it, has appeared in Cambodia. I did not think this was possible since Cambodia has a lower population," said Dr. Soliz.

"Well, what does it mean overall?" said Jett.

"More of the aliens have come, and there appears to be more of the Anomaly where the factions are," said Dr. Soliz.

"Is the Anomaly still stunning, freezing, or killing people?" said Jett.

"Yes, it is, but with a more limited frequency," said Dr. Soliz.

Jett heard some groaning, and it was Captain Meno. He knew he could no longer divert his attention from what was happening before him. Jett got close to Stan and asked Jaguar to enter his mind.

"Jaguar, tell Stan to give it all he has got. I am tired of this stalemate," said Jett.

"You know, we may not live; there are too many variables," said Jaguar.

Jett heard something in what he interrupted as another language in the distance in his mind. The orb had gone upwards, but he still wished he were on it for some reason. Stan immediately began to glow, and everything around him—including Jett—grew with this brightness.

Stan threw his hands up, held some of the Sphinxes up, and turned them around in the air. He then sent them hurling to the other end of the jungle outside Angkor Wat. Sono laughed, and more Sphinxes, by the hundreds, surrounded him.

"I know your secret, Jett," said Sono.

"And, what would that be?" said Jett.

"Not, what, but who?" said Sono. "I know someone lurks in your mind and has appeared to you. Mother Gaia, right?"

Eyeing Sono closely, Jett grabbed a plasma gun to see if he could shoot at him with it. He positioned the weapon and opened fire on Sono. The bullets went right through him. It was only a hologram.

"Sono, where are you?!" said Jett.

"I am nowhere but everywhere," said Sono's voice.

Jett looked around the nearby temple complex and jungle. Nothing was there. Stranger still, he saw some locals bowing down to a group of trees. Stan was throwing up more Sphinxes into the air, but they kept coming. Suddenly, there was a break in the line of Sphinxes, and Jett made a run for it to get to Captain Meno.

"Hold on there, guy," said Jett as he wiped some blood off Captain Meno's mouth.

"You made it, Jett. I knew you would," said Captain Meno.

"Helen was captured, and Corporal Balco and the others did not make it. We found a friend, Dr. Soliz, who helped us make it this far and to Cambodia. We also have one of the aliens' spaceships, for lack of a better term," said Jett.

"What are those things? Those things are vile, Jett! Not even Sono likes them!" said Captain Meno.

"You must understand, Captain. We have unraveled what is causing the forces, and we have caused the aliens to come, coupled with the action of powerful individuals in the governments and the Sphinxes," said Jett.

"There's no time for more understanding," said Captain Meno.

Jett stood back from Captain Meno, calibrated his plasma gun, and aimed it at Captain Meno's handcuffs. The plasma from the handgun sizzled off the handcuffs. Jett sent Captain Meno behind Stan and by the orb. Jett looked for an opening so he could take a shot at Sono.

Since Sono was nowhere to be found and his hologram flickered in and out, Jett focused on finding Helen. He looked for something to cover with and advanced on the Sphinxes simultaneously. He took cover behind the nearest enormous tree and began climbing it. When he looked down, he saw Helen in the distance. She was sitting cross-legged with Sphinx guards pacing back and forth.

He positioned his gun and aimed his plasma gun at the Sphinxes. He shot a couple down, but the rest began to open fire in his direction. Jett began to hop from tree to tree and eventually jumped to the ground behind Helen and the Sphinxes.

"Don't move," said Jett to the Sphinxes.

The Sphinxes abruptly turned around and charged their weapons. Before they could move any further, several of them were blasted with plasma. Dust and debris went everywhere, and some Sphinxes began begging for mercy. Helen ran to Jett's side.

"Jett, you made it! I didn't think you were going to," said Helen.

"We made some new friends along the way; I hope you like them," said Jett.

Jett gave Helen a stun gun, which he had around his waist. Jett and Helen moved quickly through the temple complex behind Sono. The ground beneath their feet began to shake, sending them to the ground several times. Jett forgot about Jaguar and stopped to catch his breath and communicate with Jaguar.

"So, this friend is a big cat, but in a vision form. Only I can see him. Remember those hallucinations or visions we were having. I found the source. I'll explain more later," said Jett.

Jett went to his watch, which Dr. Soliz had converted into a device to monitor the Anomaly and El Diablo. Jett found a frequency that Dr. Soliz said had been proven for Jaguar to use in communication with him. He turned the frequency on and closed his eyes.

"Jaguar, where are you?" said Jett.

"I'm here, but it looks like Earth is losing. The factions of Stan's kind are coming through more and more," said Jaguar.

Jett would have liked to know exactly how these factions and Stan's kind came through to Earth, but he knew there was no time to ponder an immense problem to solve. This time, Jett sees Jaguar and the young woman with a jade skirt he had seen on the alien ship. She is tending to the Jaguar. Her black hair was silky, giving the illusion that it was some waterfall. Jett could not help but notice how lovely she was, but he knew Helen was just a pinch away from his dream-like state.

"Who are you?" said Jett despite his thoughts about Helen.

"I'm from the sky," said the young woman.

"What do you mean, I have never met someone from the sky?" said Jett.

"But you have. You remember all those times with your family at the parks, looking at clouds and naming their shapes. You would remember me; You would remember your past," said the young woman.

"May I know your name?" said Jett.

The young woman responded in silence. She kept tending to Jaguar. And Jett looked more closely. He could tell that there were some bloody wounds on Jaguar's body, and the young woman was earnestly tending to them. After some time, the young woman looked up.

"I am tied with Jaguar, and because of this, I am tied to you," she said.

Jett was bewildered by what she said. She was talking about the past. What was she exactly referring to now, he thought? Jett felt like she knew why he had been chosen for this mission and why everything had been happening even more than possibly, Stan.

XVIII

Still fending off the Sphinxes, Stan finally suppressed them, and Jett and Helen approached from behind, armed with some of Sono's weapons. Sono had gotten to President Schimdt. Holding a gun to President Schmidt, he took the president back in a safer direction.

"Stan, what are we to do? He has the President," said Jett.

"We need to let him go," said Stan.

Jett kept his weapon pointed in the direction of Sono. Some jeeps appeared behind him and took Sono and the President. Jett felt the pain of defeat. He looked up into the sky, and the orbs of the other factions of the aliens were coming in fast into the area.

Sono was gone in a few minutes, but had left Captain Meno. Jett knew they must regroup and care for those wounded, primarily Captain Meno. Helen and Dr. Soliz rushed over to Captain Meno. Many leaves from the jungle trees had fallen to the ground.

"Stan, the factions are coming," said Jett.

"We need to get back into the orb," said Stan.

Helen and Dr. Soliz took Captain Meno into the orb. When he entered, the blood immediately dried up, and he began to regain the rhythm of his breathing. He stopped groaning and found he could stand straight. The door closed behind them, and the orb took flight.

"Stan, you didn't tell me your technology had the power to heal," said Jett.

"There are many things we can do, and there's more back in my realm," said Stan.

Helen turned and went over to Jett. Dr. Soliz played with his equipment and began sharing it with Captain Meno. Dr. Soliz had collected a lot of data, and with the fall of Command to the Sphinxes, they needed all the information they could get.

"So, tell me more about these friends," said Helen as she pulled Jett aside.

"Well, the aliens turned out to be some of our friends. I named one Stan, and he is a member of the faction that does not want to eradicate Earth because of the Sphinxes' actions. And then there is Jaguar. Jaguar is Earth. It isn't very easy, but I can communicate with Earth. We lost Corporal Balco, though," said Jett.

Helen seemed elated and overpowered at the news of the operation's friendship with the aliens. She knew that was good enough before all of this took place to complete their mission. She had learned some things about the Sphinxes, but not much.

"What about the President?" said Helen.

"That was Jaguar's idea. He said we needed to take him to stop the mayhem with the mind-controlling drugs," said Jett.

"So, the Sphinx's mission was a success," said Helen.

"We have more on our side. We have Stan, and who knows who or what he commands. We have to be careful not to start something with him," said Jett.

"Jett," said Dr. Soliz, "We need to regroup at the research labs in Seattle. Captain Meno said things will be better there."

"But the orbs, and the Anomaly and El Diablo are already there," said Jett.

"The research labs are in the surrounding countryside, and they are underground. So, we should be safe. They are operational and still have a small crew working them," said Dr. Soliz.

"I'll tell Stan about the Seattle plan," said Jett.

Jett searched the hallways, but the orb had no hallways. All he had to do was close his eyes, so he did so. He could only see color at first. In his mind, Jett searched for a connection to Stan despite their proximity in a gigantic orb. When Jett saw a forest and a clearing, he honed his senses. He separated the tall grass as he reached the end of the forest. There was Stan, standing alone in the middle of a clearing in a forest.

"Stan," said Jett, running up to him.

Stan's head was pointed down, and his shoulders were slumped. Blue, blackish, and grey colors filled Stan's body. Jett did not know what to say seeing Stan in this condition. He decided to touch him. There was nothing. A butterfly flew onto Stan's head and fluttered its wings. Jett got an idea. He took his hands and started to pull up some grass, and made a clump of dirt that he placed on Stan's shoulders and hands. He smothered the dirt into his side. Stan then raised his shoulders and breathed.

"We're losing Jett, but thanks for the reminder of Earth," said Stan.

"We're not losing, please don't say that. Dr. Soliz says we can go to Seattle to regroup," said Jett.

"The factions have taken over Seattle. We will not last long, but very well," said Stan.

"Is there anything more, Stan? You look somber," said Jett.

"It's the fact that we lost some of my kind in fighting with the factions. And, I lost someone I loved," said Stan.

"Was she pretty?" said Jett.

"We don't have sexes in our kind. But, yes, if she had a sex, she would be described as pretty," said Stan.

Stan raised his hands, and the forest and clearing fell away, revealing the order and chaos of the plasma inside the orb. Another of Stan's kind appeared, and they looked like they were directing an orchestra subtly. Before Jett, the plasma separated, and the Seattle skyline lay in the distance, along with hundreds of orbs of the factions. The Anomaly and El Diablo were also in the area.

"We have to go underground, Stan. The Anomaly is on the outskirts of the research labs. They are hidden here," said Jett, with some notes handed to him by Dr. Soliz.

The orb lowered itself near the labs. The Anomaly was sitting there, and some victims were seen. The victims stood there in their bleak, motionless scream. Jett knew it was the scream of Earth dying in secret. Looking further around him, Jett could tell no birds were in the sky. Stan still had his somber colors on, and he moved his arm above where the labs were, and the doors opened.

When they opened the main entrance to the lab, a civilian scientist was ready to meet them. He looked desperate, and his eye contact was erratic. He had not come into contact with Stan's kind yet.

"Is that an alien, sir?" said the scientist.

"Yes, but they are on our side," said Jett.

"What about the others?" he said.

"We'll debrief you in a moment," said Jett.

After debriefing all of the scientists in the labs, Dr. Soliz took Captain Meno to a lab to test some new weapons, and

Captain Meno ordered Jett and Helen to record their journey privately for a moment.

In the dimly lit lab, Jett began to write down his journey from when the military first picked him up. He was sitting just across from Helen, who was earnestly writing as well. Some scientists came over and asked if they wanted a glass of water or rations. Jett declined, but Helen took them up on their offer. After some time, Jett finished writing and walked over to a viewing area where they were sitting.

He wondered if Helen knew some of his conflicted feelings about the mission. The question of why he was picked for this mission continued to plague him, but he felt more like a fit for it after certain events, like Jaguar and befriending Stan. Jett wanted to say something to Helen about the anger that lay inside him. He knew this anger was more like rage, and he felt justified. A part of him felt like he could do something, like he would act out on this emotion. Fingering through his journal, he wrote a note on the back page. It read "Friends stick together."

Jett and Helen had been writing in their journals for several hours when Captain Meno approached them again. Jett handed the journals to him, and he patted Captain Meno on the shoulder. For a second, Jett thought none of this had happened to them.

"You look better already, Captain," said Jett.

"Your friend and his technology and ship cleaned me up real nice," said the Captain.

"Jett, I need you to help develop a plan to remove Sono. You have connections with the aliens, so you are the right man for the job," said Captain Meno.

Jett shook his head and looked down. There was a Jaguar that Captain Meno did not know about yet. Jaguar was hurting, but that was a different topic he needed to address. Right now, it was only Sono.

"Do we know where Sono is?" said Jett.

"He is in Galveston, where Command is," said Captain Meno.

Looking up, he saw Captain Meno needed someone to take on Sono. Jett knew he may not be the best, but he was the best the situation had to offer. Captain Meno handed Jett new maps of the command and where things had been stationed since the Sphinxes had run them. It was mostly the same, except for the large room and defense area hiding the president.

"Do you mind me asking where you get these maps?" said Jett.

"From the scientists here and throughout the country, there has been a little bit of a resistance movement since we were taken over," said Captain Meno with a smile.

"Well, do, Captain Meno. I'll gather up Stan and Dr. Soliz," said Jett.

When Jett arrived at Dr. Soliz's lab, he was busy with his scientific equipment, taking measurements and data from Stan. He kept mumbling to himself, and Stan looked more than elated by the colors he was given off during Dr. Soliz's procedures. Stan was an alien, alright. No one would enjoy Dr. Soliz's scientific procedures.

"Dr. Soliz, we will be leaving for Galveston in about an hour," yelled Jett over the drone of some equipment.

"Could you wait a second?! I keep making discoveries of a lifetime. Did you know Stan's kind appears to utilize its plasma sensory organs for heightened perception in the dark and in the darkness of space?" said Dr. Soliz.

Dr. Soliz took a step back from Stan. He gazed in wonder at the alien creature before him, but also realized Stan had a personality and meaning much like humans. Still engaging with Stan, Dr. Soliz took a note about Stan's piloting of the orb.

"Well, I'm done now, Jett," said Dr. Soliz after thirty more minutes of scientific investigation.

"I'll get Helen," said Jett.

They emerged from the underground labs and started to walk towards the orb. The ground shook as factions of orbs passed over them. They could not do much if the factions found them out now. As they neared the orb, the door opened, and Jett took a deep breath.

Now that they were in the orb, Stan did his usual routine of interacting with the material around him. He was one with the orb. Some of Stan's kind had stayed in the orb and had not gone into the lab. Stan said they could not part with what could be the last remnants of their way of life—their civilization, Stan almost said.

"We will be in Galveston in under five minutes," said Stan.

"Thank you, Stan," said Jett.

"I noticed that some of your crewmates—if you will—Stan are showing signs of distress," said Helen.

"They are showing signs because there may be a great loss of life. You and Jett may even lose yours, but we must proceed," said Stan.

When the orb reached Galveston, it landed on a small strip of land by a bridge. Command's center was just east, past some marshes, where the alien ship lay. Dr. Soliz had yet to confirm if it was related to the current aliens and their ship. Captain Meno was arming himself with what was left of ammunition and weapons. There were some grenades and a shotgun left. Stan, however, signaled something different.

"We should go in unarmed and cause no harm," said Stan.

"That is suicide!" shouted Captain Meno.

"My kind don't understand such a selfish concept," said Stan curtly.

"They should start because my kind are very selfish," said Captain Meno.

"I don't know about you guys, but this is all still fascinating even though death could be near," said Dr. Soliz.

Jett and Helen remained silent as they walked along the strip of land to Command. The area seemed to be deserted. Victims of the Anomaly still lined the bridge going into Galveston and on the Strand. They entered through the western part of the Command, hoping to find more weapons and ammunition. There was no ammunition, but there were some clues to the whereabouts of Sono and the President at Command.

Some rations had been left, and equipment was left on as if someone or a group were in a rush. Jett moved slowly past the area and into the center of Command. The center was vacant. It was hot and humid enough that Jett could tell the air conditioner had been turned off or was no longer working. Looking up at the ceiling, he found that the glass reflected motion. Jett held up his hand to the others. Stan was with them, and not once did Jett think about how prominent Stan's presence was, but Jett knew Stan could fight Sono and the President well.

Pointing in the direction of the motion, Jett signaled to Stan where Sono and the President could be in Command. Stan raised his hands and lifted much equipment, boxes, and other cargo from the ground. That's when Jett saw them.

With their hands raised, William Sono and President Schimdt knelt on the floor together. Captain Meno automatically grew stiff and aimed his weapon at them. Stan motioned for him to lower it.

"I told you we need to tell them we mean no harm," said Stan.

"But this is a trick," said Captain Meno under his breath.

"It isn't. They are sincere. President Schimdt is no longer on the mind-controlling substance," said Stan.

"So, you did this willingly for all of us. You sold us out. You deserve no respect or allegiance," said Jett to the President.

The President was smiling, although Jett noticed something different about it. Something frozen was in the smile. The group of them looked harder.

"Mr. President!" shouted Jett.

There was no response, but he heard Sono's laughter. Sono continued to raise his hands and laugh at everyone present. That's when he looked at the President.

"Why don't you speak up? You're all-powerful in this world," said Sono.

With that, the President fell face down with a knife in his back and blood on the floor. It was the blood of a murderer who showed no remorse. Jett was about to show no remorse for the other one as well.

XIX

elen and the others' faces were not roiling with shock, so Jett looked on at the bloody corpse. Stan stood there without movement, and his color had changed to neutral beige. Stan was Jett's favorite chameleon, and he knew Stan could trounce Sono.

"I wouldn't budge," shouted Sono.

Jett looked around and found about fifteen Sphinx thugs had entered the room with weapons in a ready position. Jett moved closer to Stan, hoping for cover. He looked up at a computer screen still broadcasting the movement of the orbs. With a sudden beep of its terminal display, Jett's attention focused on the computer. More orbs were coming. They were practically on top of them.

With no time for Sono's games, Jett moved to a better position to look outside the weapon, hoping he would not see the factions of Stan's kind. When he looked out through the window, his heart sank. There, they were firing towards the city of Houston, which was miles from them. With that fire in the sky subtly yet menacingly around them.

Some of the orbs were typically different colors. This time, they had smaller orbs circling them. The US military's return fire followed the orbs' attack. They took the bombs with ease. Their colors barely changed. They seemed to grow larger as more bombs hit them. There was a constraint in the fighting. It was not all-out war just yet.

"Stan, you need to draw Sono's attention. I'll need Dr. Soliz to man that computer terminal and figure out what is going on up in the sky," said Stan hurriedly.

"I'll bring no harm to Sono," said Stan abruptly.

"What do you expect him to do?" said Captain Meno.

"Dr. Soliz over here at the computer," said Jett.

Dr. Soliz positioned himself at the computer and connected his equipment to the data reader on the computer. He could not see more of the orbs massing outside Command. Jett noticed that Dr. Soliz had grown more tense during this ordeal.

"Jett, we need more time. A lot more time," said Dr. Soliz.

"We don't have any more time," said Jett.

"Tell Stan to do something. He's the alien," said Helen.

Stan overheard what Helen said, and his colors changed rapidly. He motioned with his arms to where their one orb was on the ground outside Command. Jett felt the orb taking flight. Following the orb with his eyes, the orb abruptly stopped south of where the salt marsh ended. It glowed brightly as Stan's color changed to red. Jett felt he still may never know what truly made Stan tick and what all his behaviors meant to the mission and life on Earth.

Their orb that went south began to dance, a behavior Jett had not seen in a long time. Jett figured this behavior meant there was no harm near other orbs. The orb continued to dance until the other orbs slowly backed away from the dancing one. They stopped firing towards the city. The US military's forces reciprocated in the abrupt ceasefire. Jett did not know how long this would last. He now knew that at least progress was being made with communication with the aliens.

Stan looked towards Sono and waved his hands in front of him. Sono immediately grew stiff, but when he did something, something was triggered. Sono had a wire strapped to him, hooked up to a steel bar. When Sono stiffened, the piece of steel flew from inside Command's building. Jett wanted to push Stan out of the way. He could not, since he had taken on Sono. The piece of steel pierced into Stan's corporeal being. Helen let out a scream, and Captain Meno let some bullets fly at the Sphinxes surrounding Sono. Gasping for air, Stan fell to the floor on his back.

"Stan!" said Jett.

"I told you to stay away," said Sono.

"Why you—" said Jett.

As Jet looked over Stan's wound, he realized the piece of steel was lodged too deeply in Stan. He ripped off his shirt and tried to cover it. Helen came over and lifted Stan's head a bit to keep him from drowning in his blood. He was dying and dying fast. Tears welled up in Jett's eyes as he realized he was losing his friend who had seen him through this journey. Captain Meno came over, covering them with some shots from his weapon.

"What's the harm done to Stan?" said Captain Meno as he ran up to them.

"Stan is hurt badly," said Helen, trying to hold back tears.

Plasma blood flowed out of his wound. He was drifting in and out of consciousness. Dr. Soliz went over to the others with his gathered medical equipment bag. There was sweat on the brow of Stan. His fiery colors were fading and being snuffed out every second or so.

"Say something, Stan!" shouted Helen.

Motioning with his hands above him, a fold opened up and revealed different areas of Earth. Jett did not know why Stan did this. Stan needed all the energy he could get while he was fighting this wound.

"There's still hope," said Stan.

"But, Stan, without you, how will we accomplish this hope?" said Helen.

Stan looked over at Jett serenely. He held his hand up and placed it on his shoulder. There was not much time, Jett thought. Jett continued to make sure there was enough pressure around Stan's wound.

"What must we do, Stan, to complete the mission?" said Jett.

"You all have been chosen, but especially you, Jett. You know what you have seen and must do," said Stan.

Closing his eyes with tears, Stan let out his final breath on Earth. Helen started to sob, scream, and pound the floor of Command. Dr. Soliz applied some Earth medicine to Stan, hoping some of the machines would revive him. None of them worked on Stan's unique non-corporeal and corporeal being.

"I have won, Jett Sanchez!" said Sono.

Jett had not felt this rage in some time. He felt the urge to do something rash, but Helen grabbed his arm and stopped him. He could barely look at the lifeless body of Stan as his fiery colors were snuffed out completely. Jett knew he must come to terms with the death of Stan, right here and now.

No silence followed Stan's death. Instead, the floor of the Command Center began to shift. The windows cracked and broke into pieces, shattering onto the floor. There were whistles in the air. They were whistles, not from birds but from an alley gone haywire. The factions that had retreated when their orb began to signal that there was no harm suddenly returned. Emitting a mournful yet wrathful hum, the orbs began pounding the area around them, yet missing the Command.

Every time one of the orb's energy pulses hit the water, the water hissed to a boil, and steam filled the beaches instead of sea foam. Dr. Soliz had a camera with him so Jett could view the outside. The aliens were coming down in troop formations to the Strand and the island's surrounding area. Jett knew what they were after and why they did not touch Command: the alien ship.

"We need to get to the alien ship at the salt marsh," said Jett.

"But, we have what we need. We have Stan's orb," said Helen.

"With no one to fly it," said Jett.

"I'll go with you," said Meno.

The temperature of the salt marsh had risen with all the explosions. There was protective equipment for this circumstance, so Jett and Captain Meno geared up and walked to the ship. The ship was slippery when it was stepped on, and it was still cool to the touch. They made it to the main room and entered their learned codes. In the center of the now-opened main room was an orb with some inscriptions on it. Jett positioned his computer scanner over the orb to decipher it, yet nothing was revealed. The blackness around them still yielded nothing but an abyss-like presence of a menacing monster lurking in its darkness.

"What are we to do/" said Captain Meno.

"We need to decipher this, right away," said Jett.

"How? We lost Stan, and Dr. Soliz is busy keeping our last orb with us," said Captain Meno.

Jett thought about everything he had encountered: Peter and his father's death, being selected by Command, and going on the mission. Something there showed him that the aliens desperately needed a *part* of him. He looked more closely at the inscriptions and found a clue. In the hieroglyphics, it looked like a thorn was piercing a hand. Jett then remembered the young woman in the jade skirt tending to Jaguar's wounds. He grabbed a pocketknife from his belt and pricked his finger. He dabbed the orb with his blood.

It gradually opened to reveal what looked like earplugs. More hieroglyphics began to appear, but Jett could easily translate them. This was a device for piloting an orb. Jett did not know why the pilots hid this specific device. He needed to know, though, to fulfill the mission Command had given him and Stan's kind wishes. When they emerged from the ship, the fire in the sky was as bright as the sun, casting an eerie glow on the ground. The area they saw now was more like seeing bleached coral on those environmental shows Jett watched as a child.

Steam crept in from the salt marsh onto the command landing platform. Jett needed Helen and the others now and access to the orb. When Jett stepped into the Command center, he saw Captain Meno holding a gun from a new weapons cache to a Sphinx's head.

"Captain Meno, what are you doing? We still must follow the instructions of Stan to inflict no harm on the Sphinxes or anyone else, for that matter," said Jett sternly.

Captain Meno looked despondent. At a closer glance, Jett noticed his face was almost marred with a tinge of defeat. Jett immediately signaled to lower his weapon.

"Captain Meno, I need you to lower your weapon. Remember, we have a mission to complete," said Jett.

"They won, Jett, but now we have them. Can't you see, we are on the winning side," said Captain Meno.

"Well, Captain Meno, you sure have impressed no one with your display of valor, or rather, stupidity," said Sono.

Captain Meno dropped the gun and aimed it right at Sono and took a shot. Sono ducked behind fallen crates, and the other Sphinxes scuttled back around Command. Jett could tell Sono was near Dr. Soliz and Helen.

"I am still going to destroy your mission, Jett. I've done it to everyone you have loved so far, and you have yet to win," said Sono.

Dr. Soliz and Helen were busy storing Stan's body for further research when Sono made a run for it and jumped on Helen. Helen whirled around and punched Sono, pushing him to the floor. Helen grabbed a weapon Sono had in his hands and aimed it in front of his face.

"I got you now," said Helen to Sono.

"Backup; I need backup!" said Sono into a communication device.

More Sphinxes gathered around Helen and Dr. Soliz. He picked up the small orb they had found and tossed it into the group of Sphinxes. The Sphinx's eyes grew wide, and they took several steps back from it. The orb began to rotate, and it lit up with an intense burst of yellow light, immediately sending the nearest Sphinx to the floor, and when the light faded, there was a pile of ash. The Sphinxes all began to yell in disbelief, but the orb kept taking them out with every moment that they tried to escape it.

The orb moved and hovered over Sono. It took a while to rotate, then it let out the yellow burst of light that even blinded Jet. For a moment, Jett thought he had died. He was on the floor about twenty feet away from where he was, and now listening to the moans of Captain Meno and Dr. Soliz. Helen immediately came into his mind.

He got up and immediately searched for the small orb. The orbs in flight above them were still pounding with weaponry. Shaking himself and attempting to bring himself out of the shock of what happened, Jett's eyes adjusted, and he found Sono had been reduced to ash. There was no time for rejoicing over the defeat of this enemy; they still had to reach the orb stationed outside Command. Captain Meno and Dr. Soliz gradually got up from where they had been stunned by the orb. Jett went over to Helen's side. She was unconscious, and Jett placed a dampened piece of his shirt on her face. She coughed for a while, then looked up at Jett.

"Jett, you're here by my side. Like I always wanted you to be," said Helen.

"What do you mean? I always have been on your side all this way," said Jett.

Helen seemed distant, like she was processing some abstract or esoteric knowledge. Her eyes welled up with tears, and her lip began to quiver. She touched Jett's face with the palm of her right hand repeatedly.

"You are going to do it, Jett. I know," said Helen.

"What do you mean? We got Sono. That's what happened. He's dead," said Jett elatedly.

Helen looked mesmerized by something, like an unknown force, that continued to enter her to keep her breathing. Touching her body everywhere for any sign of trauma or wounds, Jett set his eyes upon her eyes again. Glistening with tears of relief, she motioned for Jett to come nearer.

"Kiss me, Jett," said Helen.

Jett leaned over and kissed her, and it was a kiss he would never forget. He forgot about where he was for a while—in an almost-destroyed building with the ashes of enemies surrounding him. To a warrior, that would be cause for rejoicing, but Jett knew he had been more of a lover during this mission to Helen, always on guard for every instance he might lose her. Jett released Helen from the kiss and placed her head against the back of some cargo.

"Go, Jett," said Helen, smiling.

Jett was nervous that Captain Meno and Dr. Soliz were coming his way, but he pushed them away, heading towards the orb outside Command. Command was still being rocked by heavy fire from the factions of the aliens. Once he reached the orb, he felt a hint of recognition as he stood before it. The door appeared. Jett stepped into the realm of wispy ether. There was not much to look at inside the orb when he was inside. Jett felt he was getting accustomed to this otherworldliness of a half-corporeal and non-corporeal being. Two of Stan's kind appeared before Jett with hands opened in a gesture of peace.

"Where is he?" said one of them.

"Sono is no longer here—with us," said Jett.

The two beings' colors blazed, seeming to scream loss and abandonment. Jett felt the orb lift further into the sky, and Stan's kind took to piloting the spherical vehicle of color. Bringing a mirror-slab over, he realized he must connect with Jaguar immediately.

XX

Orange and saffron starbursts of energy bounced and intersected the orb's path as it flew into the sky. Jett waved for a mirror slab to appear in front of him. He saw the devastation that factions of the aliens were causing to the US military. It was only a matter of time before everything ended. He knew their last chance was to link up with this orb, which he believed he could do with the earplug-like device found in the alien ship at Galveston. Jett held the small devices in his hand. He figured it was time to place them in his ear.

When he placed them in his ear, his eyes automatically became fixed on the mirror-slab in an intensity that Jett had never felt. He saw no waves on the beach because the waves were no longer crashing onto the shore but turning into steam. With one shot from an orb, the sky lit up as bright as El Diablo above him. There was so much destruction that

Jett saw areas without the Anomaly. Jett's knuckles were growing white as he attempted to concentrate on the mirror-slab viewing. He waited for a connection, a whisper, or a sign that Jaguar was still alive. There was a rush of what felt like air that filled the orb. The feathered colors collapsed altogether into the staunch blackness of Jaguar.

Although Jaguar was still wounded, the young woman in a jade skirt came with him. She floated along with the filaments of light from inside the orb. Her hair wrapped itself around her body.

"You're here! Thank goodness," said Jett.

Jett's excitement was met with a darker, brooding young woman than he had first met. He did not know what to say to her. She was so lovely, but her unhappiness appeared to be deadly at the same time.

"I thought you had given up," the young woman curtly said.

"I didn't; I never have. I took care of Sono, though. He's dead," said Jett triumphantly.

"That is progress," she said.

"Helen was hurt, though, and she knows what your chosen part in this journey will lead up to," said Jaguar.

"What must I do? I'm eager to end this suffering for humanity. We still need to contact my leaders and tell them to stop and take on any remaining warlords that have taken the place of Sono," said Jett.

"Hold your hand out and let it meet mine, Jett," said the woman

Jett did so, and he felt nothing. The young woman floated there. He wondered if she was playing a joke on him. She did not look like the joking type, though. She grabbed his hand further and placed her fingers through his. Her grasp was tight, and then Jett felt the bond with Earth. At first, it was faint, but he could sense the air, and further into the distance, he could feel the wetness of the ground as they flew over areas further away. The trees were a verdant green, and their canopies hid the treasuries of deer and other animals. As the young woman drew him nearer, he could feel the crispness of the salty Gulf water further down the coast.

What Jett felt with his bond was pain and agony. Earth had been suffering and had sent Jaguar and the young woman as a plea for help and a display of strength. She released her grasp. Jaguar came up to him. He saw the deep wounds on Jaguar and touched them. Sighing in relief, Jaguar brushed his whiskers up against Jett's thigh. The wounds were still there, but Jett knew he had at least relieved Jaguar of some suffering before he passed from this life and returned to Earth.

Flying faster than anything Jett had known, Jett realized what he must do. He must take possession of Jaguar and become one with him and, with the assistance of the orb, take on the factions of the other aliens and the rest of the Sphinxes. He knelt beside Jaguar and placed his face on his.

It was with that that Jaguar slipped through his fingers like sand and faded into the manic fluid existence of the orb.

Knowing what was about to happen, Jett abruptly changed the course of the orb, to the surprise of the aliens inside the orb. He realized he had the power now, and even though Jaguar was gone, he was still with him, and they could save Earth and the world. Even though this was more than enough progress to end this suffering, Jett felt he had lost something. He thought he had lost the others and Helen most of all.

Helen knew that Jett was about to give something up, and he did. When this started, he gave up part of his humanity, guilt, and innocence of being complicit in harming the world around him. He would restore all that and help the Earth and many lives. He remembered her sweet smiles and was glad she was with Captain Meno and Dr. Soliz, who would take good care of her until all of this got sorted out. He now must signal to the other orbs that they are needlessly firing at potential allies. Jett drew a mirror slab and communicated to the other orbs to go higher in altitude so they could broadcast a message more clearly.

When the orb reached a certain altitude, they broadcasted—hours passed without a response. Jett grew nervous but knew that with Jaguar and the young woman's validation, there would be a response. As they waited, the young woman still hovered in the orb. However, releasing Jaguar's spirit brought solace to her otherwise somber expression.

"Is there anything else I should know? Before you go," said Jett.

"Many minds are hurting. The Vice President is still fighting back against other bands of the Sphinxes. Once we get a message back from the other aliens, we will go assist them," she said.

The mirror-slab pulsated, and the feathered and fluid energy that filled the orb glowed around it. The message had been received by all remaining orbs in orbit and on Earth. They are bringing down their weapons. Jett raised his hands in the air in jubilation. He wanted the others to see this now, if only Peter could see everything happening now.

They descended a bit and moved eastward. The sunset was a pale, yellow circle next to El Diablo. Jett signaled to the other aliens that he must take care of the destructive forces of El Diablo and the Anomaly. They explained to him there was a way, but it was risky considering all of the Sphinx's forces had not been eradicated.

He followed the other aliens for a while on their duties. He knew he had a lot of knowledge to consume. Their tall frames and gaunt, fiery features gave Jett solace that they were still strong. By the time they had reached Washington, D.C., it was nighttime. The desolate city lay beneath them with one outpost, the White House. The US Government had refused to abandon it because of its symbolism to the town and the country. Inhabiting the White House was their way of saying they must win.

The city was too quiet. As the orb touched down in front of the White House amidst burned cars and remains of victims, the Sphinxes came with their sophisticated weaponry. The two aliens with Jett went out of the orb with their hands outstretched, shooting out energy pulses. They struck the Sphinxes one after the other. After they disarmed and let them lie there, they beckoned for Jett to accompany them.

Jett felt his limbs. He felt alive because of the orb. For some reason, he was unsure if he would feel the same aliveness once the orbs and Stand's kind left Earth. He took a step, and his foot landed on wet cement. A recent rain had come, further washing away the debris that littered the streets. Jett followed the aliens to the White House. Some soldiers ran up to him, and he opened his hands in the aliens' gesture of peace.

"I come here for you to know we killed Sono, and there is more to this story about why the aliens came," said Jett.

The soldiers looked baffled. They took out some small tubes and snorted a substance. This took Jett and the aliens aback with their sudden actions.

"This is an anecdote to counter the effects of the mind-controlling substance," said a soldier.

"How many have it?" said Jett.

"Every soldier, pilot, and civilian assisting us, sir, has some," said the other soldier.

"What have you all accomplished with it? We still need to get rid of the Sphinxes that have turned into warlords because of this mind-control substance," said Jett.

"We have managed to push the Sphinxes back and reclaim territory, but it may be a false victory since this mind-control substance is still out there," said one soldier.

"What about other nations? Has the destruction abated in any nation?" said Jett.

Jett hoped beyond hope that their answer was yes. He hoped that Peter, Helen, and everyone's deeds and his sacrifice would not be in vain. As the soldiers gathered some information, he thought of Helen. He thought about how she could help see through some of the finer details of the mission, like she always had. The soldiers communicated some more information over their communications.

"We have more positive news, sir. May we ask who you are exactly?" said the soldier.

"I'm Jett Sanchez. I headed an operation run secretly by President Schimdt," said Jett.

"We have been looking for President Schmidt. Do you know where he is?" a soldier asked.

The aliens were growing irritated at the soldiers' questioning. It was becoming clear that the soldiers had no idea who Jett was or about any of the operations that were currently going on or had gone on. Jett again revealed the aliens' universal peace gesture. The first soldier shook his head, though.

"I'm sorry, sir, but we are going to have to arrest you for suspicion of conspiracy and treason," said the soldier.

"I don't believe you," said Jett.

"They never do," said the soldier with a sneer.

Jett was more concerned about the actions of the aliens, who were making their way to the White House despite a couple of gunshots heard in the night directed at them. Jett was shoved in the back of a military SUV. He was read his rights.

"I swear I had nothing to do with the death of President Schimdt," said Jett.

"The death—I would quit talking if I were you," said a soldier in the passenger's seat.

The car turned on, and the soldier in the driver's seat began to drive away from the White House to some distant encampment. Jett could only see because of the floodlights everywhere. When the car stopped, the soldiers got out and addressed other soldiers gathering around the SUV.

"He's coming with us," said a dark-skinned man.

The soldiers opened Jett's car door and sent him toward the man. The man had a face covering, so Jett could not identify him. An explosion rocked the encampment a couple of blocks down by the White House. The handcuffs were tight on Jett, and he wished the merge with Jaguar had given him superhuman strength.

When he looked down at what the man was carrying, he saw that the man had a large taser gun and a police baton.

Jett began to perspire. He knew his time was almost up, and he did not have many chances. Chances never existed before in Jett's world, so why now? The man tightened his arm muscles, and the taser gun fired up, and he placed the police baton in his other hand. He looked at Jett and said something in a language he did not understand. Jett refused to let his heart sink, tightened his muscles, closed his eyes, and brought forth Jaguar.